"Warm, heartbreaking and hilarious in turn...a fabulous book about love, families and making sense of life."
The Sunday Express

his book totally blew me away. I love it. It's the best new voice I have read in ages."
Cathy Cassidy, author

"A be itifully written and heartfelt novel that made ne laugh and cry in equal measure."
Watersto es Booksellers' Children's Books of the Year

"Lovely, h artwarming, funny read. I laughed out loud, nd I may have shed a tear or two."
Mich le Harrison, author of *A Pinch of Magic*

" entertaining read with a serious and absorbing story at its heart."
Books for Keeps

"i are to laugh, cry and simply marvel."
Lancashire Evening Post

"Very clever, with word play, twists, turns and great plotting. I especially loved the humour that permeates through...a rather heartbreaking premise."
Book Zone 4 Boys

"This great story is sometimes happy, sometimes funny and some parts nearly made me cry."
Toppsta reader review

"A joyous, heart-breaking and life-affirming story of one boy and his messy, muddled and madcap family."
lovereading4kids.co.uk

"The humour is wonderfully and delicately interwoven throughout the story."
Armadillo Magazine

For more information on Lara Williamson and to find a galaxy of fantastic stories, go to
www.usborne.com/fiction

THE GIRL with SPACE IN HER HEART

IN HER HEART

LARA WILLIAMSON

USBORNE

For Geraldine and Allison, with love.

First published in the UK in 2019 by Usborne Publishing Ltd., Usborne House, 83-85 Saffron Hill, London EC1N 8RT, England. www.usborne.com

Text © Lara Williamson, 2019

The right of Lara Williamson to be identified as the author of this work has been asserted by her in accordance with the Copyright, Designs and Patents Act, 1988.

Cover illustration by Julie McLaughlin © Usborne Publishing, 2019

The name Usborne and the devices 🔍 🌐 are Trade Marks of Usborne Publishing Ltd.

A CIP catalogue record for this book is available from the British Library.

ISBN 9781474921312   JFMAMJJ SOND/19   04084/3

Printed in the UK.

MABEL

Do you ever carry a lot of things around with you? I do. For example, in my pocket I carry a little silver star necklace that Mum bought me. It's supposed to be part of the constellation Canis Major, which means "greater dog". I don't have a dog, but I do have a cat called Jupiter. I'm always carrying him around too, because he's lazy and sometimes he won't budge from under my bed. I love Jupiter and I know Jupiter loves me because he keeps bringing me "gifts". Unfortunately, some of them are dead.

I have a twelve-year-old big sister, Terrible Topaz, who I'd like to carry straight into a black hole. And leave her there. Then there's Mum – I carry a little photo of her in my purse. Mum has a shop near the seafront called Fudge Fudge Wink Wink and she has a boyfriend: Galactic Gavin (by the way, it was Topaz's idea to call him Galactic and that's because she thought he was from another planet). He's actually an estate agent on planet earth though and I think he's one hundred per cent nice, even if Topaz doesn't. What's more, he loves the stars as much as me.

Finally, there's Dad, and I have a big space in my heart where he used to be. You see, after Dad went away he didn't contact me or Topaz again and Mum got sad and didn't like talking about him. When I asked her questions, she wouldn't answer and her eyes would go all misty and miserable. I don't like thinking Mum's heart was broken by Dad – even though she's got Gavin now to cheer her up. Hearts aren't ever supposed to break or have empty Dad-shaped spaces in them and that makes me worry. I worry about a lot of things. I worry about Dad not being here and how we don't fist-bump or tell each other "I love you" like we used to.

That's why the main thing I'm carrying around at the moment are worries, and they're the heaviest thing to hold. To be honest, I've been trying to keep the worries squashed down. I've tried to convince myself that I don't need to worry this much and that maybe I should ignore them. But it's not easy, especially when I can't talk to Mum.

Today, there's a whole new worry to add to my collection and this time it's not about Dad.

It's 8.30 in the evening when it happens. I'm sitting cross-legged on my starry duvet cover and busy petting Jupiter (who is licking his paws like they taste of something yummy) when my sister comes into my bedroom and plonks herself beside me. She takes a bite out of her apple and tells me that something unexpected has happened. Straight away, I know I'm about to have another worry. Topaz slowly shakes her head and sighs and tells me it's a cat.

"A cat?" I interrupt, looking down at Jupiter. "Our cat?"

"You didn't let me finish." Topaz takes another bite of her apple, then says, "It's not a cat – it's a *catastrophe* and it's so catastrophic that you need to pin back your ears." I'm about to say that pinning back my ears would be painful when she adds, "It's Galactic Gavin. He's not who we think he is." A tiny river of apple juice runs down her chin and Topaz wipes it away with her finger.

At first, I'm confused with a capital Z. Seriously, I'm so confused that I have lost all sense of the alphabet.

Not who we think he is?

Not Mum's boyfriend?

Not Galactic Gavin?

"Is he even *Gavin*?" I ask Topaz, without the "Galactic" bit that she added to his name. Already this is turning out to be a worrying situation and I can feel my stomach bubbling away as Topaz purses her lips together and then says that she doesn't know who he is. At this point, I ask Terrible Topaz if she's having a laugh.

Topaz is not. In fact, her face is as miserable as the Abominable Snowman's if he was in the desert.

"I don't understand what you mean. Gavin's nice," I mutter. In my head, the words I've just said sounded sharp. In reality, they've flopped out of my mouth like marshmallow in front of a bonfire. Gavin *is* nice though. At first, when Mum introduced him to us, I wasn't sure. He would try to smile at us and join in with conversations, even if Topaz wouldn't let him. Later on, Topaz would say to me that Galactic Gavin was trying too hard and it was a bad thing. I wasn't sure how it could be a bad thing, as Mum always said trying hard at school was a good thing. But bit by bit, Gavin kept trying. He made the day feel brighter if he was in it. It turned out, Gavin was growing on me like a fungus growing on a tree in autumn (Mr Spooner, my teacher, taught me about this).

Now I'm used to Gavin visiting and I enjoy talking about the stars with him. Sometimes he brings Topaz and me chocolate (our favourite kind because he found out what we like most in the world) and when he smiles at us it reaches his amber-coloured eyes and they twinkle like Sirius, which is the brightest star in the night sky.

Terrible Topaz gingerly nibbles the edge of her apple like a little mouse and then continues, "You're being silly, Mabel Mynt. Think about it. Not everyone is who they say they are. Some people are liars, including Galactic Gavin."

Whoah! Someone tell my sister she is more mixed up than peanut butter and jam on toast.

There's a kind of stunned silence before I insist, "You're getting this confused. Gavin's not telling us lies. I like Gavin."

Topaz wrinkles her nose then says, "Oh, Mabel. I'm not the one who's confused. And you might like Gavin, but it's clear you don't understand the games that men play."

"Like Monopoly? Or Cluedo?"

Turns out, it's not the sort of games I'm thinking about. According to Topaz, "It's the game of hurting someone and not letting them know you're hurting them, but if they did know they'd be hurt. And I know all about this stuff because my romance books tell me. They're about love and falling-out-of-love and hurting people. They're about triangles."

I blink. "I hate triangles. Mr Spooner always talks about them in maths and they confuse me. I don't get triangles at all."

Topaz's jaw tightens. "I'm talking about *love* triangles, not maths triangles. Galactic Gavin is in a love triangle and he's a liar. Let me explain..." I'm still confused, but I'm not sure I actually want an explanation. Topaz carries on regardless. "So, listen to this. Remember yesterday, when we were walking home from school and I went off because I fancied an iced bun from Bread Pitt." I nod. "Well, Bread Pitt happens to be beside Galactic Gavin's estate agency and I saw him leaving his office."

"That's hardly big news," I say, staring at some freckles on my arm like they're a dot-to-dot of the stars. "And if it *was* big news that you saw him leaving his office, then why didn't you tell me this last night?"

"Well, there's more to it than Galactic Gavin just leaving work. And I needed time to think it over and consider how serious the situation was before passing on such sensitive information," says Topaz. She looks at me solemnly. "It was a lot to take in."

"You forgot," I reply.

"*Au contraire*, Mabel Mynt," replies Topaz, speaking as though she's swallowed a French dictionary. "I did not forget. It would be impossible to forget that a woman with a blonde ponytail appeared – let's call her Blonde Ponytail Woman – and she met up with Galactic Gavin outside his estate agency and he hugged her." Topaz pauses, takes the breath of an Olympic diver and continues, "The hug was big." She swings the apple core by its stem between her fingers. "Blonde Ponytail Woman was wearing a giant coat that looked like she was wrapped in a duvet. And she and Galactic Gavin walked off down the road together."

Back up! Hold your horses! Shut the front door! "So what?" I exclaim, blowing out a long breath. "He must meet people every day in his job. He was probably showing her a house he's selling."

Topaz looks around my bedroom, saying she needs to make sure no one is listening – which is completely and utterly stupid because a) I'm listening and b) Jupiter is listening (but mainly yawning, to be fair). A string of saliva stretches inside Topaz's mouth. "Anyway, it *is* a big deal. He can't have been showing this woman around a house, because he hugged her. He hugged another woman who isn't Mum. And think about this –"

11

Topaz leans in and I can smell a puff of cupcake scented body spray. "Doesn't Galactic Gavin visit his mother on a Tuesday afternoon? Yesterday was Tuesday. This wasn't his mother. And they stopped at Throwing Rocks." I shake my head because I don't know what Topaz is on about now. "The jeweller's," she snaps.

"Oh," I swallow. "'Kay."

Topaz rises from the bed and begins pacing up and down like she's going to wear a hole in my carpet. Occasionally, she stops and seems to think about something and then marches on. "You don't understand," she blurts out eventually, her eyes locking onto me. "I never believed Galactic Gavin was right for this family in the first place and this has proved it. He is going to break Mum's heart. I'm not having Mum hurt again." Topaz fixes me with a fierce stare and I think back to when Dad left and Mum had miserable eyes and didn't brush her hair. It's hard to forget the days she sat staring into space wearing her dressing gown. I don't want Mum to sit around in her dressing gown again. I don't want her hair to look like she's rubbed a balloon on it and it's sticking straight up. I think about the Dad-shaped space in my heart and I'm aware of worry fizzing in my stomach, like someone has a straw in there and is blowing bubbles through it.

"But how will he break her heart?" My nails leave crescents in my palms.

"With lies, Mabel. Because he's not telling Mum everything. He's keeping secrets. Galactic Gavin went inside the jeweller's and Blonde Ponytail Woman waited outside and then he reappeared with a small box and I think it was a ring box." She throws herself back on my bed.

I blurt out, "Hey! How did you know there was a ring inside? Did you have a pair of binoculars?" My head begins to thump like a tiny musician is playing the drums. And I know I've lost the battle with what Topaz says next.

"Pffttt... I didn't need them. I saw Blonde Ponytail Woman take something out of the box and slap it on her finger, so I didn't need a crystal ball to tell me the future." Topaz thinks for a second, then grimaces. "Trust me. It was a ring and Galactic Gavin is getting married." She pauses, waiting to see my reaction. To be fair, my reaction is mostly me picking my jaw up from the floor. "And not to our mum. So that is why he's going to break her heart with his lies and that is why we need to look out for her."

MY SISTER

Right now, even though the atmosphere is as cold as an ice lolly in the Arctic and Topaz is glaring at me, I'd still say she might have got this wrong. You see, I know for a fact that Topaz has never really liked Gavin. Not one bit. From the first day she clapped eyes on him, she said Mum didn't need anyone else in her life, not when she'd already had her heart broken by Dad. "We don't need a Dad replacement," she'd say. "We don't need Mum to be sad again when we're fine as a family of three." To be honest, I didn't want Mum's heart broken either, but I didn't think Gavin was a "Dad replacement", because he's nothing like Dad and he never tries to be.

He's just Gavin and they're as different as cheese strings and strawberry laces. And, I like how they're different. I like cheese strings but I like strawberry laces too. That's okay.

Once I got to know Gavin, I knew I definitely wanted to give him a chance, because his heart is BIG – bigger than the Milky Way. I didn't think he could be capable of breaking anyone's heart. And he has tried his hardest to fit into our family. He's even tried to get on with Topaz by taking an interest in her romance books (she borrows those from Mum's bookshelf). But when he tried to talk to her about one of her books once, he got all confused about who was dating who and Topaz got annoyed with him and said he should stick to stars because they're less complicated. Gavin laughed and rubbed his nose nervously, but he didn't say how many billions of stars there are in the sky or how complicated they can be. That's Gavin – being careful not to make anyone feel silly.

Terrible Topaz gives me a death glare and crosses her arms; a tiny vein in her forehead ticks like the internal workings of a clock. And when she speaks her voice is so high I'm certain all the dogs within a one kilometre radius have heard her. "So, that is the catastrophe. Galactic Gavin is getting married to someone else and Mum's heart will get..." Topaz crushes her fingers into a fist and shakes her head, unable to finish the sentence.

I can tell Topaz is in one of her epic moods. To be honest she was moody before but since she started secondary school, Terrible Topaz has been like a hairdryer with two settings. One minute she's warm and lovely, and the next she blasts you with an icy wind. Yesterday she treated Mum like a jelly baby, biting her head off when Mum suggested Topaz could bring a mate home from her new school for a sleepover. Topaz said she had so many mates that they couldn't fit in her bedroom because you could hardly swing a cat in there. That's when Jupiter ran out of the room. I don't think he wanted swinging anywhere.

I know whatever I might try to say about Gavin now would be pointless because Terrible Topaz always has an answer back. And when she's in an epic mood nothing can change it. My jaw slackens and when no words come out Topaz frowns at me, insisting she saw it all with her own eyeballs and her own eyeballs are very reliable and that is why Gavin is not who we think he is. "This isn't how a romance story is supposed to go," she informs me. "By rights, there should be a big white wedding, but not to someone else. He's having his cake and eating it," she says with some authority, "and you can bet that Mum doesn't have a clue."

"Huh?" I blink, having no idea why Topaz is talking about cake now.

Meanwhile, Topaz's hands are flapping around like a flag in a storm and she eventually announces, "We don't need him. We're enough to make Mum happy."

Apparently, Topaz is looking out for Mum so her heart doesn't get squashed like a bluebottle under a newspaper. By the way, those are my words on the matter. Topaz's words were: "If she stays with Gavin, Mum's heart will be torn in two like a delicate rose petal struck by a sliver of silver lightning in a thunderstorm." Personally, I think Topaz has been reading too many romance books.

She narrows her eyes and flicks her hair over her shoulder and I just about avoid being whacked in the face. With a final flourish she declares, "I know what you're thinking, Mabel."

I swallow, wondering if she knows I'm thinking this is going to be a big worry. I wonder if she knows I'm thinking that I like Gavin and this can't be true.

Casually, Topaz walks towards the door. "You're thinking it's goodbye, Galactic Gavin. You're thinking we need to get rid of him as soon as possible. You're thinking your sister was right from the beginning. And you're correct, Mabel." Topaz clears her throat and turns to face me, her hip resting against the door frame. "I know what else you're thinking. You're thinking that your beautiful and clever sister Topaz is a hero for discovering Galactic Gavin's secret and then you're thinking she deserves a medal, or at least your share of pudding this evening."

I definitely wasn't thinking I'd share my pudding.

Terrible Topaz throws her apple core in my bin as she leaves. It hits the edge, thumps and then breaks, falling on the floor. It reminds me of a heart broken into tiny pieces. And if what Topaz is saying is true, I'm concerned my heart will break into tiny pieces too because I've lost Dad and now I'm going to lose Gavin too.

DOLLY-ROSE

The following day, I'm sitting in class, staring out the window and watching seagulls fighting over a bread roll. I'm thinking about how Terrible Topaz must have got Gavin more mixed up than a pick 'n' mix when my teacher says he has two bits of exciting news. I turn my gaze from the window to Mr Spooner.

The news is that:

1. We're discussing a new project this afternoon.
2. We have a new classmate.

Just as I'm thinking that Mr Spooner's idea of exciting isn't quite the same as mine, there's a polite little tap at the classroom door and Mr Spooner flings it open. A girl with long copper wavy hair peers into the room and is ushered inside. "Welcome to Dóchas Primary School, Dolly-Rose." Mr Spooner beams and adds, "This is your new class and we'd love to hear five interesting facts about you before you take a seat."

The girl looks around, blinks, blinks again but she doesn't smile. Instead her cheeks flush as she says that she lives in Buckingham Place. Fact one. I don't hear facts two and three because I'm so busy giggling at Lee, who is asking if she lives in Buckingham Palace. He tries to bow but bangs his head on the desk, which makes me laugh even more. Mr Spooner does not like us chuckling away when we're supposed to be listening and asks me to be quiet.

"You can't be listening if you're laughing," Mr Spooner says, staring at Lee and me.

For the record, I think it is possible to do both at the same time. But I stop guffawing long enough to hear facts four and five: Dolly-Rose's dad is a nuclear scientist and her mother is a brain surgeon. Mr Spooner urges the class to give Dolly-Rose a round of applause, which we do, and suggests that we make her welcome by introducing ourselves individually at lunchtime.

At lunchtime, I see Dolly-Rose and she looks a bit sad and I remember how Nana Anna once joined a new bowling club and she said she felt worried and nervous, which was understandable when you're starting something new. I realize Dolly-Rose might be feeling that way and I know what it feels like to worry so I want to be her friend. And that's why I'm standing in front of her now introducing myself, telling her that my name is Mabel Mynt with a "y". Dolly-Rose is sitting on the wall and she sighs, looks up from a book she's reading called *Daydreaming Daisy* and replies that her name is Dolly-Rose – Dolly like the mixtures and Rose like a flower.

Firstly, I say I like Dolly Mixtures and then I say that the houses in Buckingham Place are very nice. "I don't know anyone who lives in that road. The houses are like mansions. But I guess if your dad's a nuclear scientist and your mum's a brain surgeon then I'm not surprised. My mum has a fudge shop right on the seafront called Fudge Fudge Wink Wink. Our house isn't a mansion, even though my Nana Anna says that a bag of fudge at the seaside actually costs a small fortune, so by rights Mum should be mega-rich."

Dolly-Rose looks up at me as if I am a silly five-eyed alien wearing a tutu, which I am clearly not. "You don't know anything about my life," she mutters. For a second, there is a silence more awkward than your pants being eaten by your bottom, but I quickly fill it by saying I'll tell her some facts about Dóchas Primary since she's new here.

Before Dolly-Rose gets a chance to complain I say, "If you go into the classrooms on the first floor and stand on your tiptoes you can see the lighthouse on the horizon. And seagulls are always eating from our rubbish bins. The caretaker hates it when we put leftover sandwiches in there. We have a tree that's about one thousand years old in the playground and no one knows but me that there's a little hole in the trunk where you can hide things. I'll give you a tour of the whole school, if you like."

"Oh no, I don't think I'll be needing that tour," scoffs Dolly-Rose, setting her book down. It lies on the wall like a broken-winged butterfly and she juts out her bottom lip, before shaking her head. "I'll be leaving very soon. You see, I can't stay here long because I'm going to be a huge star." She stares up into the sky. I follow her gaze although I can't see much except a load of grey clouds.

After a few seconds of considering the chance of it raining, I turn back to Dolly-Rose and say, "I'm not sure you can technically be an actual star."

"Why not?" Dolly-Rose's eyes lock onto me and then narrow. She pauses, waiting for my answer.

I give it: "Because you'd be a big mass of gas." I meant to engage my brain before I said anything daft, but then my mouth just went *Nah, let's go right ahead* and the words slipped from my lips like syrup from a spoon. I laugh, because I've just told Dolly-Rose she'd be full of gas and it's the funniest thing ever. But realizing what I've said, Dolly-Rose's eyes turn to sharp little blades of anger and I have to bite the inside of my cheek to stop myself cackling.

"You're annoying, Mabel Mynt with a 'y'. Don't ever speak to me again," says Dolly-Rose, picking up her book and pretending to read it.

"It's upside down," I say, scuttling off.

In the afternoon, Mr Spooner is babbling on about this new exciting project he mentioned earlier. Apparently, it's a project that he's calling Poetry in (e)Motion. It's going to be our big opportunity to write emotional poetry; a chance to discover that what we see in people and the world around us isn't always the whole picture. To dig deep below the surface.

"Like if you've got a bogey, sir," pipes up a voice from the front row. "You've got to dig deep."

"Not quite, Lee," says Mr Spooner, pressing his lips

together like a drawstring bag. "We're going to write our own poems but think deeper, look deeper, write emotionally. Imagine an iceberg..."

I can tell Lee is imagining it because he's shivering.

"You only see a part of it sticking out of the water, but if you look carefully you'll see so much more below the surface. That's what we're going to do with our poems. Think *iceberg*. Think *everything is not what it seems on the surface*." Wise words from Mr Spooner, totally ignored by the class, who are watching Lee shivering and giggling. "Can you please pay attention?" says Mr Spooner. "When we're finished, we're going to write our best poems on a piece of card and attach those to helium balloons that will float away from the front of the school. Your writing can be thoughtful, funny or heartfelt, and hopefully someone out there will find your balloon and be touched by the poem in some way. Kindness costs nothing, you know." Mr Spooner grins and then hands us blue notebooks and tells us we can get started at home by keeping these notebooks and jotting down a few ideas in our spare time. "No one else has to read what you've written. Write happy or sad in there. Anything that stirs emotions and helps you dig deeper. Write what's right for you."

Lee mutters something about poetry being written by

losers. He makes the L shape with his fingers.

Mr Spooner makes an X shape with his fingers and suggests it's the mark Lee will be getting if he doesn't stop talking utter nonsense.

That night after dinner, I start scribbling a poem in the new blue notebook that Mr Spooner gave me earlier. It's a personal poem about space and it deserves to be on page one. I have called it "SPACE IN MY HEART". I've written my title in big bold letters and surrounded it with a drawing of a halo of stars. As I'm writing the first few lines, the door of my bedroom fires open. Like a bad smell, Terrible Topaz appears and lingers. When I tell her that it's polite to knock, she comes over and knocks on my head, asking if that's better, before flinging herself on my bed.

It is not better but I don't say so.

"I've just finished one of my romance books," sighs Topaz. "The woman's heart – it went da-dum-da-dum-*crash*." Topaz takes her hand and taps it on her chest to make a heartbeat noise.

"What, she had a heart attack?" I raise my eyebrows so high I swear it's like they're on an eyebrow circus tightrope.

"No, she didn't," exclaims Topaz. "Don't be daft. If she'd had a heart attack, the book would have finished on chapter twenty. Nope, the man in this book broke her heart, but it went really badly for him afterwards because she waited until he went on holiday and she went into his house and sprinkled some cress seeds on his carpet and then watered them and left."

"What good was that?"

"It grew cress all over his house. When he got back from his holiday he had plenty of cress for his sandwiches. And the woman had got her revenge on him for breaking her heart," declares Topaz. "What I'm trying to say is we don't want Mum to consider getting revenge, so we can't let her heart get broken again. I've been giving this a lot of thought today." Topaz adjusts her shirt before looking down at my notebook. Even though I slam it shut I'm not quick enough, because Terrible Topaz says, "Why are you writing about space?"

"Um...I'm thinking about going on holiday," I mumble, bouncing my knee up and down.

"Where? To space?"

As I'm considering a genius answer, Topaz throws back, "I need a holiday away from *you* – and even if I ended up on Mars it wouldn't be far enough away."

When I finish pretend-splitting-my-sides-at-Topaz's-humour, which takes about 0.01 seconds, I manage to say that the book she's been reading doesn't sound like much of a romance. Topaz defends it by replying, "Oh, it was. Because the woman eventually fell in love with the next-door neighbour. And they lived—"

"On cress sandwiches?" I offer.

"Puh-lease," Topaz snipes. "They lived happily ever after. But Mum won't be living happily ever after with Galactic Gavin. I was staring at him earlier at the dinner table and thinking that we've got to look out for Mum. I'm telling you that we need to get rid of him, Mabel. And the sooner the better. Are you with me on this? The last time I mentioned it, you didn't seem sure."

I think of how much I'd like to avoid Mum's heart being broken by Gavin and press my fingers down on my notebook cover, tapping my pen on top of it like a little drumstick. Part of me still thinks Topaz has got this all wrong. Maybe she'd jumped to conclusions. Like she was on the bounciest trampoline in the world pretending she was a yo-yo, kind of jumping. Apparently, Gavin was up to no good though and Topaz knew it. Personally, I think Topaz should give him a chance. He's kind and last week he even cleaned up one of Jupiter's "gifts" because Mum said if she saw any further mouse guts she'd scream the house down. And when I couldn't figure out my maths homework, Gavin was there and he tried to help me. When he couldn't figure it out either, he told me that whatever I did in life, I'd succeed, and I felt this warm fuzzy feeling inside. That's because Gavin is one hundred per cent nice. So how can Topaz be right about what she saw?

"But if we get rid of him who will clean up mouse guts and get as confused about maths homework as me but say it doesn't matter?" I whisper, tapping the pen. Then I think: *And who will talk to me about the stars and then remind me I'll succeed in whatever I do? Who will smile and tell me I'm as bright as Alpha Centauri? Who will be like strawberry laces when I'm missing cheese strings?*

I realize my stomach is lurching even though I'm trying to keep my concerns squashed down. I think about how much I like Gavin, but then I glance at Topaz frowning at me and remember when Mum was broken-hearted and how I tried to cheer her up but nothing would work. Back then, I'd have done anything for some magical superglue to repair Mum's heart and make it like new again. My shoulders sag when my mind turns to Dad and the space he left in my heart and I wonder if magical glue could ever heal that. Only I know it couldn't. Then I think about Gavin and how he makes me laugh and how that could all disappear too, and the worry I'm feeling spins inside me like a washing machine going round and round.

"Mouse guts and maths? Why on earth are you waffling on about those?" squeals Terrible Topaz, breaking me out of my thoughts and snatching the pen away from me. She taps it on my head like my skull is her personal drum kit and she's just getting to the big drum solo. "This is serious." She taps me again. "This is a matter of life or—"

Without thinking, I mumble, "Cress?"

"Space In My Heart"

by Mabel Mynt

I need space to think
I need space to grow
I need space to breathe
I need space to say no
I need space to challenge
I need space to be free
I need space to refuse
I need space to be me
I need space to learn
I need space to be mad
I need space to remember
I need space to be sad
I need space to finish
I need space to start
I need space for ever
But not space in my heart

THE WORRY
SUITCASE LIST

As I'm walking to school on a grey Monday morning, I think about how Mr Spooner was right about the important stuff being under the surface. I considered it all day Friday and then over the weekend and realized that I need to prove to Topaz that what's under Gavin's surface is one hundred per cent nice. For what it's worth, I don't think he *could* be marrying Blonde Ponytail Woman, like Terrible Topaz said, because he's always telling Mum he loves her. He says it every time he visits. He says it Mondays, Wednesdays, Thursdays and Fridays and weekends too. Sometimes he says it all jokey, sometimes he says it seriously, and sometimes he says it quickly, like when he waves goodbye and wanders away down the front path. In my humble opinion, you can't be in a love triangle if you truly love someone, like he does my mum.

As I turn into the High Street I convince myself that Topaz has been mistaken and maybe Gavin has a double out there who looks just like him or that Blonde Ponytail Woman doesn't even exist. When I think of Gavin I smile and convince myself that I don't need to worry. The problem is, I soon discover I *do* need to worry. On the corner of the road ahead of me I see a car pull up, and as I stare through the back window I swear I can see a man and a woman hugging – and then the passenger door opens and, to my shock, out climbs Gavin. A second later, the car zooms away and I'm certain I see a ponytail swing as the driver turns her head.

Well, I don't mind saying, my face freezes and I am glued to the spot, as if someone has placed my feet on a dollop of chewing gum on top of a splodge of superglue. "The love triangle" – the words slither from my lips. If Topaz had still been with me and hadn't already headed towards her school, she would definitely have said, "I told you so." Gavin glances along the street, but I quickly duck behind a bin, and then he turns away and saunters down the High Street, whistling, towards his estate agency, Yes Lets. From behind my bin I watch as the car driven by the lady with the ponytail disappears over the horizon, and that's when I remember Topaz's romance books, and that's when the thought that Mum might end up shaking cress seeds over Gavin's floor doesn't seem so impossible.

Eventually, after I've managed to drag my feet from the spot, I realize the smile has turned into a grimace. And I'm definitely not feeling as bright as Alpha Centauri. The rest of the way to school, I try to tell myself that this whole thing was a mirage. Mr Spooner told us mirages are optical illusions where you see something that's not there, like if you're in a desert and you see a lake. And although where we live in Dóchas is not technically a desert (although the lough is just like a lake), I suppose it's still possible to imagine stuff and be completely wrong. I mean, Topaz often imagines she's clever.

But as I wander through the school gate, I know that Gavin and Blonde Ponytail Woman weren't a mirage and now I've seen them together there's no point in pretending I haven't. So, I have a whole new worry to add to my worry suitcase after all. That's what I call it, by the way: my worry suitcase. One weekend a while ago, Mum had to go away on a work course and I had to stay at Nana Anna's house. When Mum was zipping up my pink kitty suitcase she said it was fit to burst. I said there was still room for my favourite teddy and I made Mum unzip it so I could squeeze it in. Mum smiled and said it was funny how there was always room for more no matter how full it already was. It got me thinking about suitcases and how you could always squeeze in another thing, if you tried hard enough. That's how I felt about my worries – that there was always room to squeeze in another worry and then another one... And that's how I came up with the name.

So, the worry suitcase is not an actual suitcase, because it doesn't really exist. Not like my pink kitty suitcase. It just feels like it's real. The worry suitcase is a huge suitcase I keep inside my head and I stuff all my worries in there and then I carry it around. It turned up not long after the Dad-shaped space in my heart and just before Mum started dating Gavin. I worried about where Dad had gone, I worried about Mum not talking about him. I worried about her being broken-hearted, because her eyes were as sad as a puppy dog's eyes. I worried about how she didn't enjoy making fudge and sat around in her dressing gown, staring into space.

Topaz told me she was worried about Mum too, so then I worried about Topaz being worried. I worried about things changing around me. I worried that I hadn't told Dad I loved him enough. I worried about the big things and the little things, and I shoved each and every worry into the suitcase until it was so full I thought it might explode. Or *I* might explode.

Even now I don't tell anyone about it, because I'm not sure they'd understand. Imagine if I said: *Hey, I've got a space in my heart and a worry suitcase in my head.* People would wonder what I was talking about. So, I keep it quiet. It's *my* suitcase and *my* worries. Sometimes I even worry that I won't be able to get rid of it.

Not ever...

Anyway, this is a definite new worry to add to the worry suitcase – Gavin *is* two-timing Mum, like Topaz said. I've just seen it with my own eyes. I slump down beside the school water fountain. That's when a teeny-tiny voice inside my head reminds me that Gavin *was* one hundred per cent nice but not any longer. Right now, the suitcase feels so heavy I can hardly breathe. That's the thing about the suitcase, it always seems to get heavier and not lighter. I wish I could stop worrying about everything, but the truth is, I even worry about having a worry suitcase in the first place. You see, I have a list of worries and then I add new ones to it all the time:

My General Worry List

1. I worry about Mum being happy
2. I worry about Dad being happy even though I don't know where he is
3. I worry about wanting to ask Mum questions about Dad but then upsetting her because she doesn't seem to like me asking questions
4. I worry that I have a worry suitcase and I can't speak to anyone about it because no one would understand
5. I worry about not saying "I love you" to Dad before he left because that's really important
6. I worry that I'll never say "I love you" to him again
7. I worry that I'll never see Dad again, or be able to fist-bump him
8. I worry about Jupiter killing things, because Mum doesn't like it and I worry that Mum might not want Jupiter
9. I worry that my worry suitcase will never get

lighter and I'm going to have to carry it around for ever

10. I worry that Galactic Gavin is cheating on Mum (new worry).

Once, I was so concerned about number nine on my list of general worries that I nearly told Mum about the worry suitcase. We were lounging in the living room like two lazy sloths and Mum was chatting about how heavy her handbag was getting and how she needed to clear it out because there was rubbish in there from ages ago. It was right on the tip of my tongue to say that's how I felt about the worry suitcase. And I wanted to explain that I was even having dreams about being squashed by the weight of it. My mouth opened and it felt like I was a bubble machine with tiny bubbles of words coming out but exploding before anything made sense. Mum just blinked and asked why I was opening and closing my mouth. She laughed and said I looked like I was catching flies. I didn't laugh, because I desperately wanted to tell her about the suitcase, but the right words in the right order just wouldn't pop out. I wanted to tell her I missed Dad a lot and I was worrying about him too. But I couldn't say it because I knew it would make Mum sad. In the end, Mum just smiled and said,

"I probably need a suitcase instead of a handbag." She grabbed my hand and gave it a squeeze.

I wanted to tell Mum she didn't ever want a suitcase like mine.

But the moment was gone like a bubble bursting in mid-air.

Mr Spooner is shaking his bright blue maracas with little palm trees on them. It's his way of telling us to pay attention and that we need to quieten down, because we're not even ten minutes into the school week and we're as giddy as little goats. To be honest, I didn't know little goats were giddy, but I'm just a kid, so what do I know about it? Anyway, I'm busy quietly drawing a bulging suitcase in the back of my English book. It takes up a full page. Maybe it's even going to spill onto the next page.

"Concentrate, class. The weekend is over and you're back at school," says Mr Spooner as I try to scribble a handle. Then I draw myself squashed underneath the case, with just my feet poking out, like I'm the witch in *The Wizard of Oz* movie. Holy guacamole, I think Mr Spooner must have a secret travelator on his shoes because he's moved so quickly from the front of the class to my desk at the back that I barely noticed him doing it. Now he's looking at my drawing and telling me I'm not paying attention and, what's more, I'm not on my summer holidays yet so I don't need to be drawing suitcases with little witchy feet.

Everyone laughs, except Dolly-Rose.

Mr Spooner shakes the maracas at me.

Everyone laughs again.

Mr Spooner wags his finger and then shushes everyone and says there will be consequences if we're not quiet.

We don't find out what they are because everyone falls silent.

"Good, we're not having a party here," says Mr Spooner, which is kind of ridiculous because the maracas totally suggest a party. He wanders back to the front of the classroom and adjusts his belt before setting the maracas on the desk. "I want to quickly mention Poetry in (e)Motion again before we start our history lesson. As I said before, we're going to be writing poems that'll take us on an emotional roller coaster and help us learn that what we see on the surface isn't the whole picture. Everyone should be chomping at the bit to do this project."

Lee, who has to sit at the front of the class so Mr

Spooner can keep a beady eye on him, isn't chomping at the bit. He turns around and I can see he is chomping on some chewing gum though. If Mr Spooner catches Lee he'll be in big trouble, because Mr Spooner does not tolerate chewing gum since an unfortunate incident with the school hamster and a chewing gum catapult.

"So," continues Mr Spooner, "I hope you've spent the weekend writing down little poems in your special notebooks to get some practice. I expect they're nearly full by now."

Lee snorts.

"Ah, I'll take that as affirmation. Good. But what I want to do is quickly mention a little bit of homework that'll kick off our project properly tomorrow," says Mr Spooner, pulling out a picture of a trombone which he holds aloft. "What is this?" he bellows. When we all shout, "Trombone," he says, "No," which proves that teachers know nothing. "It's a trombone on the surface, but there's a story behind it, more to it than meets the eye so to speak. This trombone was discovered after a ship called *Seas the Day* got caught in a terrible thunderstorm off the coast of Dóchas a couple of years ago – it hit the lighthouse and lost its cargo. This turned up on the beach not long after, but the rest of the cargo disappeared into the sea."

There's a gasp in the classroom. Mainly because Mr Spooner has spotted Lee chewing and is telling him to get rid of it or Lee will be in his Bad Books. For the record, Mr Spooner has Bad Books and Good Books. No one has ever seen them. It's just something he always says. But if you're in his Bad Books he tells you off or makes you write lines. Lee once had to write: *I will not make a catapult out of chewing gum and try to fire the class hamster into orbit just because his name is Comet. I will also consider myself lucky that the hamster was unharmed thanks to my quick-thinking teacher.*

"So, where was I?" asks Mr Spooner and Lee mutters, "In the classroom." Mr Spooner is now very annoyed and says Lee will be in the head's office in a minute. "Okay, so you've got the idea of what I'm expecting from you. Now for your homework I want you to find an important item that you can write about tomorrow." Mr Spooner suggests we might have a family photo at home, which would be a good starting place. "Why was it taken? Where was it taken? What is the story behind it? There must be one. Can anyone tell me quickly about a special photo?" Mr Spooner is very good at asking questions – the class are not so good at giving answers. "Okay, don't all answer at once. What if you have a special object from your mum or dad instead? Or a book which tells much more of a story than you first think. Consider this tonight – think of an item you could write about and tomorrow I'd like you to bring it in, explain what it is and then write me an amazing poem. Right, now that's sorted we're on to discussing Ancient Greece."

As everyone else groans I bristle, still thinking of the homework. My *I Need Space* book is my most treasured possession because Dad gave it to me the night he left. The problem is, I don't want to bring it in because then I'll have to talk about it and it's hard to talk about how Dad disappeared and the space in my heart arrived.

I NEED SPACE

It doesn't seem like much – just a tatty book with turned-down pages and a chocolate-milkshake stain shaped like Saturn on the front cover, but it's everything to me. It reminds me of Dad; not because he loved space – he didn't – but because he gave me the book on the last day I saw him.

We'd had a nice family day at the cinema followed by hotdogs, and it didn't seem like anything unusual, only the day ended up with Mum and Dad fighting like cats and (not hot) dogs in the kitchen. (Nana Anna always describes arguing as "fighting like cats and dogs", which is a bit silly because Jupiter doesn't fight.

He just sinks his claws in and then walks away.)

Anyway, Mum was yelling that she wasn't happy about Dad's job, which was buying and selling stuff down the market. Mum called the stuff "knock off" but Dad said it wasn't. That evening he brought out a box of books he was going to sell and Mum pulled one out and flicked through it, then asked Dad if he knew anything about Mandarin.

"Aren't they baby oranges?" said Dad.

Mum shook her head and then flung the book on the table, saying the books were written in Mandarin and did he know many people in Dóchas who spoke Mandarin and would buy all the books? I think that's when it all kicked off more than a kangaroo with itching powder in its pouch. Mum said Dad wouldn't be able to sell the books down the market and he was wasting what little money we had. Then she got *really* angry, because her voice went as high as a helium balloon on a mission to Mars. She was squealing that she was sick of Dad and his schemes to make money and she told us to go to our rooms as she didn't want us to hear the rest. Topaz did but I sat on the bottom stair, and I couldn't help but overhear them because my ears refused to stop listening.

Next thing, Mum was firing all the books down the

hallway. One landed near my toes and the force of it made my hair ripple like the ribbons on a wind-tossed kite. Dad came down the hall, shouting that Mum shouldn't throw things. When he saw me sitting there, he handed me the nearest book and said I was to go to my bedroom, shut my door and look through it quietly. I nodded and took the book and pretended to go but I stopped at the top and sat down. I rested my head on the rose wallpaper and waited until Dad went back into the kitchen before looking at it. This book was different to the others in the box. It wasn't written in Mandarin and it had a night sky on the cover – navy-blue with zillions of tiny dots of silver that shone when you moved the book this way and that. It was called *I Need Space* by P. C. Wheeler and when you flicked through the pages it felt like the universe was right there in front of your eyeballs. And there were stars on each page with writing inside where P. C. Wheeler explained what the universe meant to him personally. I stayed sitting on the top stair, flipping the pages, and then when Mum and Dad wouldn't stop shouting, I ran to my bedroom with it, glad to forget what was happening on earth and escape into all the stars in the book. Just like Dad had suggested.

And it was magical. I stared at galaxies and

constellations and billions of tiny white speckles of stars scattered across double pages and I forgot that Mum and Dad were arguing downstairs because I was in another world; a world where anything felt possible.

The next morning everything came crashing back to earth because Dad had gone and Mum said they were separating. "Like cheese strings," I said to Topaz. Topaz said Dad was nothing like a cheese string and anyway adults were always splitting up and getting back together again and you couldn't do that with cheese strings. She said I'd see Dad again in the blink of an eye. I blinked my eyes a lot but I didn't see Dad again, which made me wonder how long Topaz's eye blinks were.

It turned out Mum and Dad didn't get back together. Not ever. And when I asked Mum where Dad was and if we could visit him, she told us she didn't know Dad's address. It hurt like a splinter in my heart. Dad had gone away and I wanted to tell him how much I loved him. You see, Dad and me always had this special routine at bedtime. He'd tell me the same little story about a special rock overlooking Dóchas lough. On clear evenings Dad said you could stand on this highest rock, overlooking the water, and if you wished for it hard enough your worries would float away like dandelion clock seeds. Then he'd give me a little fist bump and tell me to let my worries float away. I'd laugh and he'd say he loved me and I'd say it right back. Sometimes, if Topaz couldn't get to sleep, she'd climb in beside me and Dad would tell us both the same story. Topaz loved the story too but she couldn't have loved it as much as I did. Now, I didn't know where Dad was and I worried about him being happy. But I worried about more than that. You see, within one worry there can be lots of other little worries. So, not only did I worry about Dad being happy:

I worried if he was okay.

I worried about where he was living.

I worried that he might not have a home.

I worried that he had a home but didn't want me in it.

I worried that he might forget me.

I worried that I didn't tell him I loved him.

I worried that he didn't love me.

I worried that the worries could never float away.

I worried that I'd never fist-bump anyone again.

So the space book reminded me of Dad and that last evening with him and it was important to me. I read it from cover to cover about a hundred times. I even wrote to the author, using the publisher's address on the front page. I wrote Dear Mr P. C. Wheeler... I wanted to give him his full title, because I thought it sounded better than P. C. Wheeler. And Nana Anna said it was polite to address a letter to Mr, Mrs, Miss or Ms. Then I told Mr P. C. Wheeler how I loved the stars and I wanted to be an astronomer just like he was and then I asked questions like: How can I become an astronomer like you? What is an astronomer's favourite sweet? What is your favourite type of telescope? And then I asked him why we feel so connected to the stars.

A couple of weeks later I got a short letter back from P. C. Wheeler's publisher and it was on navy-blue paper and the words were written in silver ink – like they were written in trails of stardust. The publisher said they were replying on behalf of P. C. Wheeler and these were the answers to the questions I'd asked. They were as follows:

a) You could start by doing work experience in a local observatory when you're old enough.

b) They're partial to a bit of fudge.
(Yes, I was disappointed, because I wanted it to be Milky Way.)

c) SKYVIEWER 2020.

d) The reason we feel so connected to the stars is that humans have the same kind of atoms as the rest of the galaxy – essentially, we're made of stardust.

It blew my mind right there and then (although a tiny part of me wished P. C. Wheeler himself had signed the letter).

Anyway, what I'm trying to say is that even though my book is my most important object, I can't bring it into school with me. I glance up at Mr Spooner, who is waffling away about Ancient Greece. No, I think, I can't explain about my book. Because if I answered one question, another would follow and then suddenly Mr Spooner would be trying to get all the information from me. Sometimes I think teachers are in the wrong job and they should be detectives, quizzing criminals, because the baddies would blurt out all the answers straight away.

Nowhere in my mind do I want to tell Mr Spooner how Mum threw my book down the hallway when she was fighting "like cats and dogs" with Dad. And I can't face saying that Mum and Dad separated and Dad never came back, leaving Mum with a broken heart and me with a space in mine. What's more, I can't tell everyone in the class how much I stress about stuff and how I wish Dad would walk back up the garden path to tell me my usual bedtime story, tuck me in and tell me he loves me.

No, I can't say that at all.

THE GOBLET OF TRUTH

The next morning, Mr Spooner asks us to bring out our important objects and place them on the desk. Three times this morning I got into a complete flap and considered putting my space book into my school bag, only each time I felt my stomach somersault and then fall splat at my feet. The last time it happened, it felt so bad that I looked down to check that my stomach wasn't *really* on the floor. And that's when I saw something move under my bed – it was Jupiter's claw and there was a bit of metal glinting beneath it. Now, I'm no Einstein, but I was pretty sure Jupiter hadn't found a golden mouse. When I eventually prised the object from his claws, I saw it was a tiny golden goblet that looked like a shiny pottery teacup with two handles but was smaller than my palm. Even though it looked like gold, I guessed it wasn't anything special. Not if Jupiter had found it. But I figured it might be easier to write a poem about the goblet rather than the book.

That's why I'm looking at the golden goblet right now.

Mr Spooner sails down the aisles of the classroom saying, "I'm prepared to be amazed and astounded by your objects." He stares at Lee's mobile phone as he passes his desk and says that Lee had better have a good explanation for why it's important. Lee smirks rather than uttering a word.

"What did you bring in, Dolly-Rose?" I lean over to ask her. The thing is, I'm trying to be extra-nice to Dolly-Rose because she's still quite new. And kindness costs nothing, according to Mr Spooner. Although I wish I hadn't bothered speaking, because if looks could kill, I'd be like one of Jupiter's "gifts" right now.

"Why are you always prying into my life?" hisses Dolly-Rose, setting down *Daydreaming Daisy*, which is the same book I saw her reading at lunchtime on her first day and the one she's been secretly reading under the desk this morning. "That's the second time you've done that since I started here." When I say I can't even remember the first time, she reminds me I was talking about Buckingham Place and that where she lives is none of my business. Dolly-Rose's jaw tightens and then she sighs, "What important item did *you* bring in anyway?"

I swallow down an invisible golf ball and feel my eyes prickle with unformed tears. Technically, I didn't bring in an important item. I brought in a golden goblet that means nothing to me. When I don't answer, Dolly-Rose glares at me and then at the golden goblet, which I quickly push under my pencil case.

Abruptly, Mr Spooner shakes his maracas, which gets everyone's attention. "Are you all dozing back there? This was a great homework assignment and I'm looking forward to hearing all about your items." I'm not sure those two words "great" and "homework" go together. Neither do "exciting" and "project", or "maths" and "fun", but Mr Spooner is always spouting on about these things. "It's over to you now."

His heat-seeking-laser-missile eyes start searching the room. They sweep left. They sweep right. This is always a scary moment for anyone in the class. He is searching for a victim to go first. I think about going first to get it over with, then I think about avoiding eye contact and making myself invisible so the teacher won't pick me. Then I consider making eye contact in a "double-bluff", hoping that if I look keen Mr Spooner will think I *want* to have a turn and then he'll avoid me. Then I think if I keep my head down long enough in the hope of going last, maybe Mr Spooner will run out of time. I'm deciding on which option is the absolute best when Mr Spooner calls out my name.

My mouth drains of saliva like a burst paddling pool drains of water.

It was a stupid idea to bring in the golden goblet, because I can't think of an emotional story to go with it. My whole body has turned into a worm, wiggling and squirming with embarrassment. Mr Spooner repeats my name like I didn't hear it the first time and then he asks if there's another Mabel in the room. I think this is more of a rhetorical question. According to Mr Spooner, that's when a question is asked for dramatic effect without expecting an answer. "I presume you've brought in an object." Another rhetorical question. "On your feet!" That's just a command, right there.

I'm on my feet. My feet don't want me to be on them, because they're wobbling like I'm on stilts made of jelly. Slowly, I pick up the small golden goblet with trembling fingers. At the front of the class, Mr Spooner urges me not to be shy, which translates in teacher-speak to: *Hurry up and get to the point because we haven't got all day*. At this stage, all I can think about is how I found a tiny golden cup under Jupiter's claw and it seemed like a bright idea to throw it in my school bag instead of my *I Need Space* book. Right now, I don't have a clue what else I can say about it. A bazillion thoughts run through my head and none of them are any help. With hands shaking like I'm playing an invisible tambourine, I hold up the tiny goblet for everyone to see.

Mr Spooner picks up his glasses from the desk and puts them on the end of his nose and then he makes a funny little whoop of delight and asks me if it's what he thinks it is. To be fair, I have no idea what he thinks it is. A second later Mr Spooner glides over to my desk to inspect the tiny cup, sucking all the air through his teeth and making these little noises of appreciation. He turns around and tells the class that I am clever beyond my years for having an interest in this subject. He says I am brilliant. This *is* brilliant. Everyone is grinning except Dolly-Rose, who is bristling like a bristly hedgehog with a bristle brush on its back. And Lee, who is picking his nose with the corner of a ruler.

Mr Spooner asks if he may borrow the goblet and before I can answer he scoops it up in his palm and

walks up to the white board and writes in marker pen:
LIES LIES LIES.

I choke and then try to disguise it and when Mr Spooner asks me what's wrong I say I have something in my throat.

"I imagine that's your larynx," Mr Spooner says, shaking his head. He places the marker behind his ear before adding, "So this goblet has an interesting tale to tell and it involves…" He taps the interactive whiteboard and the word **LIES**.

At this stage my face feels hotter than a barbecue on the hottest day of the year. And Mr Spooner's eyes narrow and he says that if I'm not ready to talk about the object yet then he's more than happy to do so. My head just bobs by itself. Mr Spooner gives me a happy grin and says there's absolutely no need for me be nervous, but he'll do the talking anyway. With that, he walks over to his bookcase and picks up a book called *Myths, Mystery, Magic* and runs his sausage fingers over the pages before nodding knowingly. For a second Mr Spooner reads silently, tapping his lips, and then he slams the book shut, returns it to the shelf and saunters to the front of the class.

With a triumphant smile, Mr Spooner says, "So, I just need a ruler for a second to measure this little cup, because it's supposed to be no bigger than five centimetres." Lee hands Mr Spooner his ruler. No one mentions that he had the corner of it up his nose a second ago. Mr Spooner measures the little goblet. Handing back the ruler, Mr Spooner dips his head. "It's the correct size…it all seems right. Now if you look very closely, you will see an engraving and it says *Rún*. That's spelled R-U-N but pronounced 'roon'."

While Dolly-Rose is stewing in her own annoyance beside me, I'm perched on the edge of my seat, waiting to hear more – and Mr Spooner delivers. "This little goblet that Mabel brought in is very interesting. Hold onto your hats, because this is an intriguing tale that'll make the best poem."

By the way, you can't do that – hold onto your hat if you're not wearing one. But if I did have a hat I'd be gripping it right now, because I can't wait to hear what Mr Spooner is going to say.

"Many moons ago, probably not too far from here, in an emerald isle similar to this, in a place where there was a lough surrounded by rocks and trees probably similar to the lake we have here, there lived a man called Rún. He was a magic man, someone fair-minded and noble." Mr Spooner clears his throat and holds up the tiny cup. Everyone's gaze follows it as though it's a golden snitch. There's a dramatic pause before Mr Spooner continues: "Rún had many magic objects like swords and invisibility cloaks, so the story goes."

"An invisibility cloak, I want one of those," shouts Lee. Mr Spooner stops abruptly and says he'd like Lee to have one sometimes and there is another way to make him invisible and that is to send him out of the classroom.

Mr Spooner continues, "So, where was I? Yes, Rún had all these magical items in his possession, but none was as special as a goblet that he found near a lough – the Golden Goblet of Truth. Then when he died the goblet left his hands and where it went and who took care of it afterwards, no one knows. Now, those of you who are paying attention will note that I wrote *lies* not *truth* on the whiteboard."

"But why, sir?" Lee hoists up his hand.

Mr Spooner smiles and puts a finger to his lips. "The goblet is supposed to crack three times – each time it hears a lie, it cracks." Mr Spooner makes a cracking noise with his mouth. "Lie number one, *crack*. Lie number two, *crack*. Lie number three, *crack*." Mr Spooner explains that this is why he wrote **LIES LIES LIES** on the whiteboard.

"Cups don't crack when they hear lies," says Lee

matter-of-factly. He rolls his tie up like a Swiss roll and then slumps back in his chair.

"Normal cups don't," whispers Mr Spooner, building up so much suspense I can hardly wait to hear the next part of the story. He winks. "But this one might just be magic..."

REVEALS AND HEALS

I don't mind admitting, my hearing has gone as fizzy as a super-sour fizzy sweet dipped in fizzy pop. Did Mr Spooner just say that the goblet might be magic? The goblet Jupiter found?

The myth of the Golden Goblet of Truth is hands down the best story I've heard in class. It even beats the story Mr Spooner told us about a Viking who cut off an enemy's head and hung it as a trophy on his saddle, only he got grazed by the head's teeth and then died from an infection.

"So, the goblet cracks three times when it hears three lies...but it also mends three times when it hears three truths," Mr Spooner continues, wandering back down the aisle with his tie fluttering behind him. "Just like magic."

I glance around and a few people look stunned. Dolly-Rose is one of them.

Lee puts his hand up and an exasperated Mr Spooner points to him. "But sir, what's the point? What happens when it mends for the last time? It's just a plain cup again."

Mr Spooner inhales and puffs his chest out. "Ah, but is it a plain cup again, Lee? You tell me." Lee shrugs as Mr Spooner goes on. "It reveals and heals. So, it reveals three lies, which will break your heart, but then hopefully it will reveal three truths, which will heal your heart again." Lee sucks in air, which is hardly surprising because we're all doing that. "However, don't be mistaken in believing that the cup will definitely mend. It may not. Perhaps you could be left with a broken heart for ever." Mr Spooner frowns and then gives a lopsided smile. "It's just a myth though. Some will believe the story, some will not. A myth is what you make it." He goes back to the bookcase and picks up *Myths, Mystery, Magic* again and thumbs through it. "There is a chapter here on Rún and that's what I was checking before I told you the story. Now, I don't imagine this is the original mythological goblet but if you found it, it could have the same magic. It might still reveal and heal a heart. What do you think?"

Heal a heart. The phrase echoes around the class and when I glance across at Dolly-Rose I see her mouth the words over and over and her eyes are like two glazed doughnuts. Suddenly there's a big *WHAM* as Mr Spooner slams the book shut. He gazes around. "It's a good myth, eh? Not sure how true it is though – you'll have to make up your own minds if this goblet holds the same power as the original one." He picks up his maracas and gives them a little celebratory shake and there's a ripple of applause from the class.

I lean over and whisper to Dolly-Rose, "My cup has got to be magic, that's what I think. Did you see how excited Mr Spooner was? I'm so glad it's mine." Oh, how daft I was to think that it wasn't all that special. I can see now that this golden goblet is very special indeed. I'm not sure where he found it but Jupiter has brought in a bit of magic that can heal a heart – I didn't know that was possible. If Jupiter was here I'd ask him where the goblet came from and then I'd kiss him for finding it (although not on the mouth because it is the mouth of a killer).

Dolly-Rose turns to me and hisses that it's a stupid

cup and not even the real thing and she wouldn't want it anyway, because everyone knows myths are made up and a silly cup can't heal anyone's heart.

Oh.

But when Mr Spooner passes the goblet around the class for everyone to get a look, Dolly-Rose holds onto it for ages, rubbing it with her finger, holding it up to her eye and inspecting it. Reluctantly, she passes it on. Eventually, the goblet returns to me and Mr Spooner thanks me for bringing in such an amazing object that reminded him of the myth. He even gives me a gold star. Obviously, I am in Mr Spooner's Good Books.

A few seconds later, Mr Spooner saunters back to my desk and hands me the copy of *Myths, Mystery, Magic* and suggests that before I write my poem I might take a minute to read the chapter on Rún's magic goblet, since I'm so interested in it. "To be honest, I didn't know you were a fan of myths." Mr Spooner grins at me.

"Oh yes," I reply and then I look at the cup in horror in case it knows I've just lied, but luckily there's no crack.

"Good-o," says Mr Spooner. "Have a read of this and enjoy, but make sure to return it." He claps me on the back and there are a few thoughts in my mind: *Lee's snot was on the ruler, Mr Spooner's hand was on the ruler, Mr Spooner's hand is on my back. Lee's snot is on my back.*

Myths, Mystery, Magic:

The goblet was once one of Rún's special items, along with a sword and a cloak. It is said in legend that the cup will detect three lies and three truths. But be warned, one cannot seek to force the cup to work. Nor pretend-lie to it, because it will not perform as you'd wish it to. No, rather the goblet will discover the lies for itself, as it will discover the truths for itself. Accept the cup as it is, since leaving the hands of Rún it belongs to no one. Although the person who has found it may use its power wisely; allow it to perform magic in its own time, do not rush it. Take care of it, share its wisdom with others, let it spread magic, hoping that one day it might heal a heart. Some may ask, how will you know if it has healed a heart? You will simply know and that is the true magic.

"Pfftt... Did you just tell me you've got a magic cup? Who are you, Aladdin?" snorts Topaz, who is waiting for me as usual at the school gate. She pulls the zip up on her coat and mutters, "You know there's no such thing as magic, right? I mean, you don't actually need to believe in fairy tales or myths or whatever that daft teacher of yours tells you. Sometimes, Mabel, I wonder why I even bother coming to walk you home from school when all you do is tell me stupid stuff like this."

I shove my hands into my pockets and start marching ahead, saying, "You don't have to walk me home. And I believe my teacher. Anyway, it's all part of this project we're doing called Poetry in (e)Motion. We're going to write a poem about looking at something below the surface. Like an iceberg."

"I wouldn't want to look too deeply at stuff, that's what I think. Sometimes it's easier not to bother and take things as you find them."

I pause before pulling the goblet from my pocket and sticking it under her nose. I say that even if Topaz doesn't believe in magic, I bet she'd like to know more. Wafting the goblet round I say that the magic is strong in something so tiny. A low sun reflects on the gold and as it shimmers in the light Topaz tuts.

"Ugh! Your tacky goblet looks like something the cat dragged in. There's nothing about it that interests me."

I almost say that it *is* something Jupiter dragged in,

but before I get the words out Topaz wafts her hands around as if she's swatting invisible flies, saying the goblet is silly and babyish and to get it away from her.

"Well," I reply, "wait until you've heard the whole story first." When I tell Topaz what Mr Spooner said and what I read about the goblet in a book, explaining that it reveals lies and truths and that it might heal a broken heart, her ears prick up. "Reveals and heals," I declare.

Topaz breaks into a villainous smile. She snatches the golden goblet from my hand and squints at it, tilting it this way and that. "Ooh, it's quite small," she muses. "But pretty," she continues. "Magic, you say? Detects lies, you say? Proper lies and truths?"

Trying to grab the goblet back, I argue, "You're not interested in magic, you don't believe in silly babyish things like this. Topaz, give me back the cup."

"FYI," replies Terrible Topaz, her voice all sing-song as she makes sure I can't reach the goblet, "I'm taking care of it for now and using its power wisely. So I *do* believe in magic, if it can help us."

"Help us?"

"I've got an idea. It's a shame Galactic Gavin's not at ours tonight – but I'll just have to save my brilliant idea for tomorrow when he turns up." Her face glows as if I've just shoved a golden nugget under her chin. Then

Terrible Topaz pops my magic goblet into her pocket and walks off, saying that as sure as there are millions of stars in the sky, she's going to get to the bottom of this business with Gavin and Blonde Ponytail Woman. "I'm going to use this magic cup to prove that Galactic Gavin has a girlfriend and that he's lying about it," says Topaz.

"Billions," I correct her.

"Billions of girlfriends?"

"No, stars in the sky," I reply. The worry about Topaz's plan appears almost instantly. I add it to the worry suitcase, because there's always room for one more worry. Always...

"The Golden Goblet of Truth"

by Mabel Mynt

I have a cup of purest gold
It's in my hand right here
It's full of magic, I've been told
And that is what I fear

For Topaz thinks a lie will come
And she has got a plan
And Gavin will not find it fun
If he's the lying man

And if the cup cracks once or twice
She'll know that it is true
That Gavin isn't very nice
And he will make Mum blue

And this could be a muddled mess
Right from the very start
It makes me sad, I must confess
That lies could break our heart

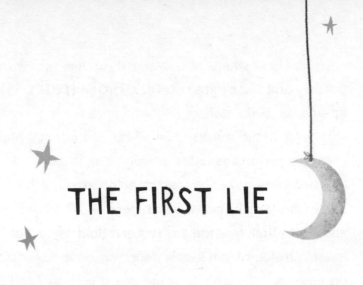

THE FIRST LIE

My bed is like the world's comfiest cloud and the walls in my room are navy-blue and dotted with silver star stickers. My bookshelf is above the bed and it's full of books including my important *I Need Space* book. It is the book I always reach for. I reach for it when I'm happy or sad, when things are quiet or loud. I reach for it when I want to escape or when I'm worrying. Sometimes I lie on my cloud bed and imagine that I'm floating in the sky and I get off my cloud and dance in the stars, flicking each one with my toe and scattering stardust everywhere.

Even though my bedroom is perfect, I sometimes

have dreams where I'm trapped under the worry suitcase and I can't get out. On nights like that I wake up and lie in the darkness, thinking that I'll never be able to leave the suitcase behind me. If I cry out, Mum always comes in and tells me everything is okay. I don't tell her about the suitcase or the dream though. Sometimes I wish Dad would come in and fist-bump me and remind me that the worries can float away, but he doesn't. Instead Mum kisses me gently on the head and promises me she's here for me and she always will be because that's what parents are for.

Not always.

Not Dad.

I'm lying on my cloud bed when Mum calls me for dinner. I get up and go downstairs. Today is Wednesday, which means three things:

1. Bolognese
2. Gavin
3. Terrible Topaz's plan to use the golden goblet to prove that Gavin has a girlfriend.

Gavin is nearly two metres tall and it looks like there's a giant sitting at our kitchen table with a piece of garlic bread clamped between his fingers. He grins at me, revealing this little gap he has between his two front teeth. Grinning back, I sit down beside him as Mum offers me some garlic bread and then places the basket in the centre of the table. Gavin bites into his garlic bread and butter squirts out, and I laugh. He looks at me as he wipes the butter away and says he'd "butter be more careful next time," and that sets me off laughing again.

Terrible Topaz's face is so hard it could crack concrete though; instead, she's gnawing on a bit of bread like a dog chewing a bone. She sets the romance book she's been reading on the table and then reaches into her pocket and pulls out the tiny golden goblet. She places it in the middle of the table beside the sauce bottle. "Oh, this is all very funny," says Topaz drily, her eyes locked on the goblet. "But I guess it's easy to be laughing all the time when you get to have your cake and eat it."

I remember the last time Topaz mentioned having cake and eating it. It was when she told me Gavin was going to break Mum's heart because she'd seen him with Blonde Ponytail Woman. I swallow and glance at Topaz before looking at Gavin.

Gavin takes another bite of garlic bread and shrugs and says he didn't realize we were having cake but if there's cake he's always happy to eat it. His eyes twinkle but Mum looks concerned and says there isn't any cake and tells Topaz it's ice cream for pudding. Vanilla. Topaz tuts and says plain old vanilla is boring and then she continues to Gavin, "I bet you like to have different flavours, don't you? One isn't enough. I bet you're the sort of man who has two scoops. Two, not one."

I know what Topaz is trying to say and I shake my head, hoping to put her off. It doesn't.

"So, Gavin," she goes on. "One is boring, yes?"

Now I'm hissing at Topaz to stop and she's ignoring me and Mum is leaning across the table, asking me why I'm hissing.

"It's an animal impersonation. I'm a snake," I answer.

Topaz mutters something under her breath that sounds like "More like a mouse, you coward."

"Well, can you do your snake impersonation later – preferably in your bedroom when you're alone? Because you're spreading saliva over the garlic bread." Mum narrows her eyes.

From this point on, Terrible Topaz is on a one-girl mission to prove that Gavin is telling us lies. She peppers him with one question after another. She asks him where he was yesterday afternoon and he says he was visiting his mother as usual, and then she asks him where he was last Tuesday and Gavin echoes that he was with his mother then as well. He was there the Tuesday afternoon before that and the week before that too.

"I leave work at around 3.45 to see Mum and I don't get home again until about six o'clock," says Gavin, matter-of-factly.

Topaz raises her eyebrows like an evil egghead. Then she asks about triangles. "What do you think of those, Galactic Gavin?"

Gavin looks a bit perplexed, either by the question or the fact that Topaz has just called him "Galactic" or because a piece of spaghetti is refusing to stay on his fork. He twizzles his fork, hooking spaghetti like little worms, and folds everything into his mouth and chews.

Gavin swallows. "Not going to lie," he replies, which makes Topaz sit right up, "I like cheese triangles. I sometimes have one in my lunch box."

I laugh, but my stomach turns into a Catherine wheel and I can feel the worry batter against my insides.

Topaz glares at me and she's like Medusa in Greek mythology – the monster that Mr Spooner told us about who could turn you to stone with a look. "Forget triangles. So, you *always* visit your mother on Tuesdays? You never do anything else. Is that right?"

Of course, I know exactly why Topaz is saying this. It's because she saw him with Blonde Ponytail Woman on Tuesday last week, which meant that Gavin was not with his mother.

Gavin, who doesn't understand the importance of the question, nods. Topaz gives me a look, then stares at the goblet and mouths "lies" but nothing happens. The goblet doesn't crack, much to Topaz's annoyance. Unaware of what's going on, Gavin turns to Mum and says it's good that Topaz mentioned him visiting his mum and it's about time Mum met his family. Mum smiles and says she'd like that and then they start talking about work. Gavin's waffling on about houses and Mum about Fudge Fudge Wink Wink and how most tourists like trying fancy flavoured fudges. Undeterred, Topaz asks Gavin if he likes just one type of fudge or if he likes two. What she's trying to ask him is if he's got two girlfriends not one, but she won't come out and say it straight. And now Gavin is talking about fudge and cake and eating like it's his second favourite subject in the world (the galaxy being the first).

"Excuse me," Topaz continues, butting into Mum and Gavin's conversation and leaning so far over the table that her school tie is nearly in a puddle of garlic butter. "I'm not even talking about fudge." That's when it happens. Finally she blurts out, "Would you ever tell lies?"

"Topaz," snaps Mum, raising her eyebrows. "What sort of question is that? Don't mind my daughter, Gavin. She can't help being rude."

Uh-oh! The worry of all this is sending my heart rate sky-high. Gavin is looking confused, while Topaz's eyes are firmly on the goblet, locked onto it like Jupiter locks onto his prey. Then Gavin smiles and tells Mum he doesn't mind answering. He says he wouldn't unless it was a little white lie so as not to hurt anyone.

Terrible Topaz is fuming because the goblet still hasn't cracked and Gavin's not telling us one way or another. "Mum doesn't like lies, do you, Mum?" she says pointedly.

Mum frowns and I expect her to explode in annoyance, but instead she blushes and mutters something about agreeing with Gavin. Then she gets up to get some grated cheese.

"And would you ever consider buying a ring for a woman?" hisses Topaz.

"Any woman?" Gavin blinks and from where I'm sitting I can almost feel the heat of a fireball whooshing up into his cheeks.

Topaz waits, tapping her wrist, even though it looks stupid because she's not wearing a watch. Blustering,

Gavin informs us that yes he would, but we'd be the first to know.

"The first to know? *Would* we be the first to know?" We all watch as a tiny missile of spit fires from Topaz's mouth and lands on Gavin's plate right in his last forkful of bolognese.

"Yes," Gavin assures her, glancing down at his plate rather than meeting Topaz's eyes. He looks disappointed that he can't eat the last bit of his dinner and then he says he needs to go to the toilet and he'll be back in a moment. With that, the conversation is completely closed down, but not before Topaz gives me a kick under the table. I kick her back, only I miss and my toe connects with Jupiter, who nearly scratches my shins to ribbons.

"We got him," hisses Topaz later when she joins me outside. "Hang on, what are you doing out here anyway?"

"I was looking for shooting stars," I reply.

"Well, you can stop that right now because this is more important." Topaz shows me the Golden Goblet of Truth. "Look." Terrible Topaz points to the tiniest hairline crack in the goblet, which I'm sure wasn't there before. Her eyes are glittering like two disco balls. "I left this on the kitchen table and went to the loo and when I came back it was lying on the floor by Jupiter's food bowl and now it's cracked. Galactic Gavin was lying. This is the proof. I told you he saw Blonde Ponytail Woman on a Tuesday when he was supposed to be visiting his mother, and that he gave her a ring." Terrible Topaz draws herself up to her full height, puts on a witchy voice and says, "He said if he was giving someone a ring, we'd be the first to know. We weren't. He lied. The magic goblet has spoken."

"It cracked," I whisper, chewing on my lip. "It *is* magic." Part of me is excited that the goblet has worked...but deep down I know it also means that Mum's heart is in terrible danger.

THE SPHERICAL JIGSAW

I wonder if it's possible to not like the magic goblet. Don't get me wrong, I like the idea that it's magic, but not the idea that it's proved Gavin's cheating. For the next five minutes I try to convince Topaz that the goblet is probably on the blink. You can't totally rely on one crack in a cup. The whole thing is just a myth. It's probably all made up. It fell off the table and cracked – that's how it happened. Or Jupiter might have stood on it, if it was by his bowl. To be honest, I'm not so excited by the Goblet of Truth now. Not if it's going to be used against Gavin.

Topaz informs me that she doesn't want to rain on

my chips but I can stop trying to explain reasons why it has cracked when she's now certain the cup is magic. She also says I shouldn't go around saying it's not working, because "It might hear you." She clutches the goblet to her chest, as though protecting it from my words. "Anyway, don't worry. I'm not going to rely on just one lie. The cup can reveal more. Wouldn't it be interesting if it revealed further lies to us? Maybe we could discover another lie from Galactic Gavin. I mean, the cup is very useful. I think we need to treat it well."

"But I don't want to discover more lies from Gavin. I don't want to discover any lies at all." My eyes rise towards the stars above us and I mutter, "Gavin has always been good to Mum and us. He gave me a poster of the solar system last week."

"Oh, he gives you some tiny thing—"

"It's not tiny," I interrupt, my eyes firmly fixed on the pinpricks of light. "It's the whole solar system."

"So what? He gives you the solar system," continues Topaz. "It's not like he gave you the earth or anything."

The truth is, I don't want to think badly of Gavin and I definitely don't want to have to let him go. I've hardly admitted it to myself before, but Gavin's here and I want him to stay because even though he's not Dad, he *is* fun.

I remember what happened when Dad disappeared.

I tried talking to Mum about it but she kept looking like she might cry. So I secretly texted him, thinking that if I contacted him myself Mum couldn't be sad about it because she wouldn't know. I wrote: *I love you, Dad*. But there was no message back. Dad didn't say he loved me and it was like I was texting into a black hole. I wanted to tell Mum but I couldn't when I hadn't mentioned it to her in the first place.

When it was Dad's birthday I wanted to send a card saying: Without you, Dad, I feel blue, so on your birthday, I say I love you! But there was no address to post it to. Instead I wrote a little note saying Happy birthday, Dad and then I love you. I buried it under a tiny plant in the garden but Jupiter peed on it and I felt sad. And the Dad-shaped space in my heart remained.

It was still there when Gavin appeared in our lives. Gavin was definitely not Dad – he was at least ten centimetres taller for starters. Tall and thin like a strawberry lace. But Gavin didn't have to be Dad – I liked him because he was Gavin. He didn't make up for the space in my heart, but he made me laugh until my belly ached and he told me all these facts about the galaxy, like that about one million earths could fit inside the sun, and you probably couldn't walk on Jupiter because it has no solid surface.

"I wouldn't walk on Jupiter anyway," I replied. "Because he'd claw my legs off."

Gavin laughed. I laughed. Gavin was always joking around. He made me smile until my jaw ached and he made Mum happy too.

Now Topaz is telling me that I can't listen to Gavin talk about the solar system. "What's the point in talking about the universe when it's what's happening on earth that's important?" she says. "And you can stop giggling at his feeble jokes. They're not even funny. I'm the oldest and I say we have to stop him breaking Mum's heart – I've told you this a million times."

I don't think it is a million times, even if it feels like it.

My insides twist like a broken Slinky. When something feels right, why should it be wrong? "Gavin must've made a mistake," I say. You see, I still want to believe Gavin's one hundred per cent nice with all my heart – even if the Goblet of Truth is telling us he's a liar and even if I saw him in a car with Blonde Ponytail Woman. Even if Topaz is trying to convince me that Gavin is the worst person in the universe. I'm about to add we can't judge Gavin just yet, because he's innocent until proven guilty, when I hear footsteps.

"What mistake?" says a clear voice behind me. It's Gavin. He's as chirpy as a canary in a singing competition, so I'm certain he didn't hear what we were saying before. Topaz tells Gavin that's for us to know and the golden goblet to find out and Gavin's eyes ping-pong between us. Then he shakes his head and says he's getting old, because he doesn't understand all the sayings young people have these days. Apparently, in his day everything was "cool" and "ace" and "lush", Gavin tells us. Topaz snorts and says in his day it was horses and carriages and pea-soupers.

"I'm not that old," says Gavin indignantly as Topaz pushes past him. She says she's got to go to her bedroom to watch paint dry.

"Nail polish," she clarifies, before disappearing into the kitchen with my Goblet of Truth still in her mitts.

When she's gone, Gavin asks me what I'm doing outside. I tell him I'm looking at the stars and he laughs and says we're two peas in a pod then. His eyes flick upwards, gazing at the night sky in awe. Billions of flecks of light are dancing on black velvet above us. "It's phenomenal," murmurs Gavin. "It makes me feel like a dot on planet earth. Do you ever feel like that too?"

I nod, blowing warm air into my fingers.

"The sky is so vast. The beauty, the magic and the mystery. It makes me feel like I'm totally connected to the universe," says Gavin.

"Me too," I whisper. "It's because we're made of—"

"Stardust." Gavin finishes the sentence for me.

It's like he knows the words of P. C. Wheeler and that makes me so happy.

Gavin clears his throat, cranes his neck further and stares for the longest time in silence. And it doesn't feel awkward. Sometimes when there's a silence you try to fill it, but I don't right now – I'm too busy allowing my eyes to drift across the heavens, skipping over stars like a skimming stone.

"I think of it as a giant spherical jigsaw," murmurs Gavin. "All fitting together to make one perfect picture." Dancing from foot to foot to get warm, I ask him what would happen if a piece ended up in the wrong position; like it's supposed to be in one area but it goes somewhere else. Gavin pauses and then tells me the sky might look slightly different but it would still be beautiful.

I shrug.

"For instance…" Gavin mulls this over for a second. "If Canis Major was positioned somewhere else, it would still be Canis Major, wouldn't it? And the same for Orion. It wouldn't stop being Orion just because the pieces were a bit jumbled up."

That makes me think of how jumbled up my life is feeling right now. "But what would happen if Canis

Major had no address and we didn't know where he'd gone. What if his piece had disappeared completely? And what if Orion came along and that was okay for a bit, but then it turned out Orion was something you didn't expect and he was lying." I know I'm talking about Dad and Gavin. Dad is Canis Major and Gavin is Orion. "I mean, what if I really liked Orion and he turned out to be a black hole?"

Gavin laughs and says Orion isn't a black hole and perhaps we shouldn't worry so much about the spherical jigsaw after all and just drink in how amazing it is to be here, right at this moment, enjoying the wonder. I feel my body shiver and Gavin leans over and for the first time ever he pulls me into a hug and the warmth of it takes me by surprise. And the other thing that takes me by surprise is that for one tiny second it feels like all my jigsaw pieces *are* in the right place.

Then something makes me look up and I see the curtains twitch and Terrible Topaz is at her bedroom window, her fingers pressed against the glass, creating tiny Os of heat. I know she's furious. She glares at me, her eyes like subtraction signs, and I immediately pull away from Gavin's hug and the jigsaw pieces scatter again.

THE GAVIN-IS-A-CHEATER CLUB

The next morning when I ask Terrible Topaz for the Goblet of Truth back, she says she wants to hold onto it. She's standing in her bedroom with one hand placed on her hip and the other swinging my cup like it's a tiny pendulum. "Seriously, Mabel. I'm the most sensible, so I need to keep this kind of magic and look after it."

"But it's mine," I snap back. The goblet dangles in front of me and my eyes follow it as Topaz swings it back and forward.

Topaz shakes her head and reminds me that the cup belongs to no one and anyway she's using the goblet's power carefully. "You've seen for yourself how it cracked after Gavin talked about the ring last night. I love this cup."

Trying to grab it back, I shout, "I'm telling Mum you've taken my magic cup."

"Oh no you're not." Topaz pulls the cup away and gives it a slobbery kiss before turning to me. "You wouldn't mention it to Mum because she'd want to know why it's magic and then you'd have to explain that we're using it. Why can't you face it, Mabel? The goblet has proved Gavin's a liar and I bet it proves it again and again. He is nothing but heartbreak."

I draw myself up to my full height and say, "It clearly states in *Myths, Mystery, Magic* that although the cup belongs to no one, the person who found it, which is me, needs to use the power wisely. I bet it won't work properly, if I don't have it. But I am happy to share its wisdom, okay." I'm hoping this will be enough to convince Topaz.

And it is. Topaz looks disappointed and reluctantly hands me the cup back, but makes me promise that we'll use it again. "You don't want to see Mum hurt again, right? In fact, shouldn't *she* have the goblet if it's her heart that's being broken by Gavin?" she asks, her voice softening.

"No, I found it and if I don't look after it, it might stop working completely and then Mum's broken heart would never heal. Not ever." I think for a second that it was technically Jupiter who found it but I'm pretty sure he won't care if it cracks or not.

"Right," replies Topaz. "But we can still help Mum with it though, can't we?"

I mutter, "I guess, we're just letting it spread its magic." I still don't want to believe that Gavin is trouble and a liar beneath the surface. And when I get back to my bedroom I draw an iceberg to prove that he's nice. The top half has points I know about Gavin (what's on the surface) and the bottom half is things that I think about him (what's under the surface). This is my iceberg diagram:

Name: Gavin Bickerstaff
Nickname: Galactic (thanks to Topaz)
Height: Gigantic
Mouth: Gappy and happy
Age: Ancient
Works: Yes Lets
Eats: Like a hungry horse
Wears: A lot of dark blue suits with bright ties

Tries to fit in
Rubs his nose when he's nervous
Treats Mum well and he's kind
Doesn't mind cleaning up after Jupiter
Makes me feel special and listens to me

My mind is all over the place at morning break. How can the little golden goblet have worked so quickly? I stare at it, tilting it this way and that, gazing at the tiny crack. "Right, Mr Goblet of Truth. I suppose you're magic and that's good, but could you have fallen off the table and cracked? Or could you have cracked but made a mistake?"

"Talking to yourself, are you?" Dolly-Rose trots past me like a little show pony, her plaits flicking. Seeing the goblet, she stops dead in front of me and turns. "Why are you looking at that thing? I don't care what Mr Spooner said about it being magic, it doesn't work, you know. Nothing mends broken hearts. Sometimes it's hard to stop being sad if you're sad. And I should know."

I stare at my goblet, ignoring her. Just because Dolly-Rose thinks she knows everything, it doesn't mean she understands about this. And I get how starting something new can make you sad or worried like Nana Anna said but I've tried to be her friend, even when she isn't friendly back.

"It's rubbish," she sneers. She pulls a cherry lip balm out of her pocket and swipes it over her lips before returning it to her blazer.

Annoyed now, I lift my goblet up and show Dolly-Rose the first crack. Her eyes widen and I say, "You don't know everything. Look at this. The goblet *has* cracked and that means someone was telling a lie and this proves that it's working." I don't mention that a few seconds ago I was thinking the goblet must've fallen off the table and cracked. "I'm telling you, it's going to mend hearts all over the place. It will make everyone happy." Even I know I sound ridiculous because I'm exaggerating so much. "No one is ever going to be sad again. Less than twenty-four hours with this goblet could sort out everyone's problems."

"Less than twenty-four hours? No one will be sad ever again?"

"Oh yes."

Dolly-Rose blinks.

"I think you'll find that this is the best thing in the whole of Dóchas."

Dolly-Rose's eyes lock onto the goblet.

"And I'm going to keep it in my blazer pocket. Maybe

it'll make all my dreams come true. I'll get everything I want," I add.

Dolly-Rose says she's not fussed because she's got absolutely everything she could ever want already. Her eyes drop to the floor. Then she adds that even if she wants anything else, she can have it.

"You can't have my goblet though," I say smugly.

It is four o'clock and Terrible Topaz has called a meeting in her bedroom. The meeting is mainly about how she's started reading a new romance novel. I do not call that a meeting. I call that torture. After Topaz has banged her dressing table with a hairbrush to declare the meeting open, she states that this is the Gavin-is-a-Cheater Club. Next, she explains she's been reading a book and there's a serial cheater in it.

"Why? Does he eat cornflakes but then Rice Krispies too?"

"Not that sort of cereal," hisses Topaz. "Serial with an 's'."

Anyway, apparently this book is about Summer and she's got a cheating boyfriend who she lives with but who is moving a secret girlfriend into their house when Summer is away visiting family. "The secret girlfriend is called Autumn," says Topaz gravely. Her head bobs down in sympathy. "Summer is going to be broken-hearted."

"Doesn't Summer know about Autumn at all then?" I can't even believe I'm getting involved in this. "I mean, when does she find out that her boyfriend is a serial cheater?"

"Not yet," says Topaz. "Anyway, the reason I called this meeting is because I think Mum's like Summer and Gavin's a cheater and we should go to his house and check there's no Autumn secretly living there."

"Ooh, I'm not sure," I answer.

But Topaz convinces me that we've just got to rule it out. Then we'll know one way or another. "So, it could be a good thing to discover he's living on his own and if he is then we can strike off worrying about it. Rule it out."

Topaz has a point. I don't need any new worries. Last night I was worrying so much I couldn't get to sleep. My head became muffled and I convinced myself that I'd never be able to fist-bump anyone ever again and then I got sad about it and my eyes started leaking and my pillow got soggy and I had to turn it over but then the other side got soggy too so I got up and looked at my *I Need Space* book and instead of counting sheep I tried to count the stars in the picture and that made me tired.

"But we don't know his exact address," I add, blinking.

Out of the blue, Topaz grins at me and then says, "Oh, that's easy-peasy. I know where we can find the exact address and I know how we can we kill two birds with one cat." I stare at her blankly. She clarifies, "Nana Anna says you can kill two birds with one cat or one stone or something. Anyway, I think we need to discover more about Galactic Gavin." She looks at me slyly before adding, "We're going to look deeper, below the surface, like that project you're doing."

Ten minutes later, we're downstairs and Mum has spilled all the beans on how Gavin has taken the day off work because he's doing something important. When Topaz asks what's so important, Mum says she has no idea and they don't live in each other's pockets. Topaz says she's glad because she wouldn't want anyone living in her pocket. Mum says no one could live in Topaz's pocket because it's far too full of rubbish.

Then Mum tells us that Gavin won't be visiting us tonight because he's running errands later, and that means it's a night in watching whatever we like. "You can pick a movie, girls," says Mum brightly. "And there will be snacks."

"Not fudge," groans Topaz.

"Not fudge," says Mum.

"Can we watch a film about love?" asks Topaz. "And about love triangles?"

Mum says she doesn't know any movies about love triangles and Topaz mutters it's a shame and then whispers in my ear that we're living in one anyway. I push her away and Topaz grimaces and Mum tells us to stop bickering.

Then Topaz whispers to me that she's got a clever idea. An idea it is, but clever it isn't. To Mum's surprise and mine, Topaz says Jupiter needs a walk. Mum raises her eyebrows and looks a bit gobsmacked, and not in a good way. She says it's highly unusual to take a cat for a walk as they tend to take care of themselves. I'm so shocked by Topaz's stupid suggestion that I do my best goldfish impersonation, which is one hundred per cent better than the snake I did at the kitchen table.

"It's not that unusual," argues Topaz, bobbing up and down like a unicorn inflatable on a stormy sea. "It's very important, Mum. We're chaperoning him when he goes outside. It's to make sure he doesn't bring home any more gifts for you." She puts the word "gifts" in inverted commas with her fingers.

Mum's about to protest and then it's obvious she remembers the mouse guts and she gives a little shudder. Topaz goes on to discuss how the bits Jupiter brings in reminds her they're dissecting things in science and she takes us through the whole process and I think she's laying it on a bit thick and I give her a nudge and then she says, "We'll be back in time for tea though and we promise that Jupiter will not bring back any 'gifts' this time. You have my word. We will watch him." Mum's still a little unsure and that's when Topaz says she can't be stuck in her own home. "It's like being in prison," wails Topaz, flinging herself on the sofa.

Mum's mouth slackens. "Um...yes, go, do go...um... don't be long." We're at the front door when Mum calls after us, "Are you going to take Jupiter, then?"

"Jupiter? Oh, I'd forgotten about him," whispers Topaz.

GAVIN'S HOUSE

"What kind of daft idea was that?" I say, stalking down the road. At this point, I am not happy and Topaz is going to know about it. "I thought I'd never get Jupiter out from under the bed. And I had to borrow Mum's oven gloves because he was resisting. If I hadn't put them on he'd have torn my skin to shreds. And he's in the front garden now so if Mum looks out the window she'll see him there." I ask Topaz to hold onto the goblet for a second while I take off the gloves and put them in my pocket.

"Chill your beans." Topaz shakes her head and takes the goblet from me. While I'm saying I like my beans hot, thank you very much, Topaz interrupts, "Anyway, I don't think it was a stupid idea to use the cat as a cover. You didn't have any better ideas, so someone had to come up with something. And we're here now so I think I did a good job." She pretends to blow on her fingernails as if she's clever but I notice they look all bitten and horrible. When she sees me staring at them she quickly puts her hands in her pockets.

Yes Lets is a building on the High Street with a big glass front and lots of photos of houses to buy or let in the window. There's also a big sign in the window saying, LIFE'S A BEACH WHEN YOU LIVE IN DÓCHAS, SOAK UP THE SUN IN A HOUSE THAT IS FUN. WE CAN HELP! To the left is Iron Maiden, the ironing service shop, and Bread Pitt, the bakery, and a few doors down there's Throwing Rocks, the jewellery store. We've never been inside an estate agency because we aren't old enough to buy a house.

It seems our mission to discover if Gavin is secretly living with anyone is a-go-go.

The bell tinkles as we walk inside.

"Hello," says a man sitting behind a desk. "Just browsing?" He snorts and throws his hands behind his head as if he's sunbathing, which is totally ridiculous because we're in the middle of autumn. "For the day when you're actually buying a house?"

Topaz glances at a house that costs squillions and says she might purchase this one when she's a billionaire, like in one of her romantic novels. The man takes his arms down and starts tapping something on his computer keyboard. Topaz stares at another picture of a house before trotting over to him. She sets the Golden Goblet of Truth on his desk, which surprises me.

"Um...that's not going to buy you a house. You'll need more gold than that," he laughs and two of his bellies wobble a bit. The other two wobble a lot.

"Do you have an address for Galactic Gavin?" That's Terrible Topaz – straight to the point.

"Who?" The man looks at Topaz and I'd say his face had only one thing written across it: *I'm confused*. Topaz says, "Gavin Bickerstaff," and the man rubs his chin. "Oh, Gav. I didn't understand the Galactic bit. Yes, I have an address for him but I'm not giving it out. He's got a day off. Now, if you want to buy a house then that's a different matter."

"I want to buy Gavin's house," says Topaz firmly. I admire her confidence, even if it does come across as abrupt.

"I don't think it's for sale," says the man, his voice as blunt as a broken pencil. "Those houses on Chaucer

Road don't become available very often. Although I sold one last week to a couple and their twenty—"

"Children?" Topaz looks surprised.

"Tropical fish," replies the man.

There's a glint in Topaz's eye. Apparently not content with the address, she goes on, "Do you know anything about Gavin Bickerstaff buying a ring for someone special? I bet you two chat about stuff when you're in the office. Maybe he bought a ring for his girlfriend? Did he tell you?" Terrible Topaz is staring at the goblet, her eyes bulging. I know exactly what my sister is up to.

The man runs his finger under his collar and says it's a bit warm in here. Then he says, "No, he didn't," before clearing his throat and grimacing.

Already I'm picking up the goblet from the desk but as I grab Topaz by the arm I manage to drop it on the tiled floor. I quickly grab it and drag Topaz towards the door. To make things better I say politely to the man that I won't be signing up for a mansion today, thank you very much.

When we get outside I glare at Topaz. She glares back and snatches the goblet from my hand, saying, "It's cracked again, Mabel. *Lie numéro deux*. Tick." Like saying it in French is going to help matters. She continues, "I think that means that two lies have been revealed. That man said 'no' when I asked if Gavin had mentioned his girlfriend and a ring. He was lying because the cup has just cracked and confirmed it. Oh, I bet Gavin talks about Blonde Ponytail Woman all the time at work. This goblet is a little genius."

"But I dropped it," I mumble. "It probably cracked then. It's the same sort of crack as the time I dropped one of Mum's teacups."

Topaz says I need to stop trying to explain the magic.

As we look back, the man inside the estate agency is scratching his bald head and this time the look on his face says: *What on earth just happened and why did those two girls come in asking about someone called Galactic Gavin?*

Chaucer Road is on the way home, not more than ten minutes from our house. It's a narrow street, the houses standing shoulder to shoulder like toy soldiers. All the gardens run into each other and the windows have criss-crosses on them like the lattice on the top of Mum's chicken and leek pie. I tell Topaz we have no idea which house belongs to Gavin so this is a wasted mission.

"I think not," says Topaz, pointing down the road. My eyes follow her gaze. There's a red car outside number thirteen and on the side it says Yes Lets in big white letters. "I think that might be his house," she says, stroking her chin.

Anyway, that's not the only thing that's parked outside the house. There's a white van with the words **JEAN CLAUDE VAN MAN** on the side. The door of the van swings open and a beefy man in a T-shirt jumps out and whistles to his mate, tapping the side of the van at the same time. The beefy man opens the back doors and shouts, "This is the place! Number thirteen." His weedy friend appears and beefy man makes him lug out a giant armchair while he fills in some paperwork.

We're watching the little guy nearly buckling under the weight when we get bad news, bad news and more bad news. Firstly, my mobile bleeps and it's Mum. She's cooking dinner and telling me how Jupiter is in the kitchen playing chase – why isn't he with us? The second bit of bad news is that he's playing chase with a mouse. The third bit of bad news is Mum's burned her fingers because she's lost her oven gloves. Oh, and there's another bit of bad news, because Mum's next text is all in CAPITALS and she's saying WHERE ARE YOU? I EXPECT YOU HOME IN TEN MINUTES.

"Text her back and tell her we're busy," hisses Topaz. But before I get the chance, she ducks down behind a hedge, pulling me with her and lifting her furry hood up to peer out. "We need to blend in or someone will spot us," she explains. Of course someone will spot us – Topaz's school uniform is maroon and she's wearing a coat with a big furry hood and I've got a massive bulge in my green coloured blazer pocket where I've shoved a pair of oven gloves. I'm not sure that peering over the top of a hedge is going to help that much.

"We're totally disguised," I manage sarcastically, but Topaz tells me to shush because she needs to see what's going to happen next. Although I do not see how me talking affects her eyeballs seeing. Anyway, what happens next is that the front door opens as the weedy man tries to get the armchair up the pathway. He's huffing and puffing more than a steam train climbing a mountain.

"I can't see Galactic Gavin," whispers Topaz. Hmm… maybe that's because she's got her hood up.

When I pull Topaz's hood down her mouth makes an O of surprise. Following her gaze, I'm surprised too. Standing in the doorway is none other than Blonde Ponytail Woman and she's holding this big box in front of her and directing the puny man and the armchair to come inside.

"Stick that in the kitchen, Gav won't mind," she shouts.

"Stick that in the kitchen, Gav won't mind," echoes Topaz as we wander back down the road. Judging by her scrunched-up face she's annoyed because the front door shut and we couldn't see anything else. At the time Topaz wanted to ring the doorbell, but then she decided no, because the goblet is supposed to reveal one more lie and she wants to know what that is first.

All the way home Topaz is going on about how Gavin is just like the man in her romance book. "He was cheating on Summer and she fell for it. In the beginning... Autumn moved into his house and when she found out about it Summer left him. Happens every time, whenever there's a love triangle. Someone's in and someone's out." I'm about to say it's like "the hokey-cokey" then, but I don't bother since Topaz is in the mood from hell. Anyway, she's waffling on so much about how love triangles end in the worst possible way that I can't get a word in edgeways, backways, sideways or anyways.

I hoped this mission was going to rule out someone living with Gavin. This has just made things a million times worse. I now have a new worry to add to the suitcase: *Gavin is living with Blonde Ponytail Woman.*

Right now, the worry suitcase is heavy and my knees are buckling as I drag myself home, listening to Topaz complaining all the way. I think of Dad and how, if he was here, my worries would float away on the breeze and Mum wouldn't have had her heart broken and I wouldn't have the space in my heart. And Gavin wouldn't even exist in our lives.

Well, Dad's not here and my worries aren't floating away either.

Instead they're in the world's heaviest suitcase in my head.

And it's making me feel miserable.

Less than an hour later I'm at home lying on my bed. Jupiter's in a bad mood with me and Mum's in a bad mood with me because she had to clean up a mouse before serving dinner. And she wanted to know where we were. Topaz said it was all my fault because I wanted to go to the park to play on the swings. Then Mum wanted to know if we knew where her oven gloves were.

"In Mabel's pocket," said Topaz.

"Why?" replied Mum.

Topaz looked at me as if she expected me to come up with a great answer.

"Um...I thought I'd picked up my usual gloves," I muttered.

Mum blinked and asked if my usual gloves were normally kept in the kitchen drawer.

THE APPOINTMENT

The following morning, when I go downstairs into the kitchen for breakfast, Mum shoots me a look and asks if I didn't sleep too well. I don't tell her I had a dream about the worry suitcase last night. And I don't mention how it fell on my shoulders, making it hard to breathe, and then I heard the clink of the garden gate and looked out to see a muffled shape coming up the path. Even in my dream I swore it was Dad, only I couldn't see his face, and he reached out to try to lift the suitcase off me. But then I woke up, only to remember that Dad is gone and the suitcase is still here. As heavy as ever.

"Yeah, I slept all right," I mumble in a voice so flat

it's like it's been under a steamroller.

Mum looks tired too; her hair is like a bird's nest in a wind tunnel. I grab a slice of toast and put chocolate spread on it and take a bite, staring at Mum. She's got her pale pink dressing gown on and is sipping from a cup of tea and saying that we shouldn't take too long to eat our breakfast. When Topaz tries to slurp down her milk, Mum looks at the clock on the wall and tells her she doesn't even have time for that. "Come on, chop-chop," says Mum, urging us up from the table. "You should be off to school." When we get into the hallway, we pick up our bags and Mum opens the door and kisses us both on the cheek but her eyes skip away.

We're five minutes down the road and heading towards school when Topaz slaps me on the forehead.

"Ouch, what was that for?" I squeal and Topaz tells me she was going to slap her own forehead but figured it would hurt too much. Next she tells me she's forgotten her lunch box and she blames Mum for rushing us. She makes me trudge all the way back to the house with her moaning and me moaning about her moaning.

Topaz quickly bombs down the path and turns her key in the lock while I wait at the garden gate. It's quiet for a moment and then I can hear her shouting, "Hello," at the top of her lungs. When Topaz reappears, her face is flushed and she tells me something weird just happened. She closes the front door behind her. "Mum wasn't downstairs when I went in." Topaz tucks her hair behind her ear. "She came downstairs a few seconds later and she wasn't in her dressing gown. Her hair was brushed and in a little bun and she was wearing that white blouse with the big black bow. It wasn't her usual stuff for the fudge shop."

Inhaling, I ask, "Why was she dressed like that?"

"I thought it was for a funeral but Mum said no one had died. I said the mouse died last night and Mum said I was being silly and she wasn't dressed for a mouse funeral. Probably right, because when Mum buries the mice she usually wears her old clothes. Anyway, she said it was an appointment and she'd be home when we get back from school. And then she told me I wasn't a quiz master and I needed to stop asking questions."

I shake my head. "Appointment? What appointment?"

Topaz tuts and replies, "I don't know. She didn't say. But Mum always tells us if she has an appointment." Topaz thinks for a second and then adds, "She was in a bad mood too." I feel like saying, "And you should know."

As we turn right, a school bus pulls up alongside us and some of the girls on it start battering the window and sticking their tongues out at Topaz. When I ask Topaz if they're her friends because they're wearing the same maroon uniform and look like they're the same age, she pretends she can't hear me before telling me she's got to hurry to school. She pulls up her furry hood, even though it's not raining, and sprints off. She doesn't even say goodbye.

I drag my feet along the pavement, past the shops and the park, and then I take a turn into the road where our school is. That's when I spot Dolly-Rose across the street. She's talking to a group of people while holding the lead of a little black pug. She bends down to give the dog a scratch behind the ears. It pokes out a rose-petal tongue and Dolly-Rose straightens back up. I wonder if she walks her dog before school, which is what some of my other friends do.

When I get into school I wait for Dolly-Rose to appear in the playground and then run over to her and excitedly tell her that I love her dog and I have a black cat and he's called Jupiter. "He's the colour of midnight," I say, wondering why Dolly-Rose didn't mention her pet in her five facts when she introduced herself. "And he's a lot of fun, except he brings in stuff. Mum says they're 'gifts'. They're not the sort of gifts I like. They're usually dead. He brought in a mouse last night. Mum dressed like she was going to a funeral this morning and my sister thought it was for the mouse. But it wasn't. Mum said it was an appointment."

Dolly-Rose blinks and her face is as blank as a piece of paper in a snowstorm.

"The mouse ended up in the garden anyway," I say, very pleased with myself that Dolly-Rose and me are being friendly now. "We have a lot of mice in our garden. It's a mouse graveyard. Although that's not technically correct, because there are a few dead birds too."

Dolly-Rose blinks again.

I breathe in and add, "What I'm trying to say is my pet is black like yours." Dolly-Rose shakes her head as if she doesn't have a clue what I'm going on about. "What's your pet called?"

Dolly-Rose's face fogs over with fury and she tells me she doesn't have a pet, then she kicks me in the shin. And as soon as it happens I have one thought in my head: *Kindness costs nothing*. Well, if Mr Spooner was here he'd see kindness just cost me a painful shin.

In morning lessons, I lean over and tell Dolly-Rose I didn't mean to annoy her in the playground and yes,

I'll probably survive despite my poorly shin. Then I say that if I had a black dog like hers I'd be happy and take it for walkies in the park and pick up its poo and teach it to give me a paw. Well, maybe not so happy to pick up its poo. I'd leave that to Topaz. I ask Dolly-Rose again what her pet is called and Dolly-Rose says she doesn't have any pets, big or small, and then pretends she can't hear me. After that she scribbles a note on a piece of paper before holding it aloft. It says SHUT UP!

I scribble a note back and hold it under her nose. It says I WILL NOT!

SHUT UP! Dolly-Rose holds up her note again.

I scribble another note and hold it in the air. YOU SHUT UP!

"I WILL NOT SHUT UP!" Mr Spooner says, seeing me wave my note around. His eyes shrink back to tiny hamster droppings. "Mabel Mynt, please do not hold up a note telling me to shut up." I want to say it was for Dolly-Rose but I know that would still make him angry. Instead I try to make myself invisible, which is tricky when you're wearing a bright green uniform. Mr Spooner says, "Save your energies for our Poetry in (e) Motion project. I've explained quite a bit already, but what I haven't done is show you how other children have completed this project. I hope it'll inspire you and help you understand how we view others and the world around us. You see, we make judgements very quickly – perhaps in as little as seven seconds. I'm asking you to think for longer, to gain a better understanding. What you see is not always what is going on if you scratch the surface." Mr Spooner claps his hands together so loud I think he might have burst my eardrums and then goes over to the interactive whiteboard and starts playing a video of some smiling children doing the same type of project.

At the end there's a picture of them all standing holding a rainbow of balloons with poems attached. One child reads her poem about how a butterfly felt when it was a caterpillar. Another has written about how a sheep that looks different doesn't fit in before realizing it's actually a goat.

"Hey presto," says Mr Spooner, like he's a magician – only without the magic.

"They're just balloons though," says Lee. "If I wanted a balloon I could go to the precinct and buy a stupid unicorn one off the balloon man."

"Shush," says Mr Spooner. "They're not any old balloons. They're moving in two ways." Seeing our quizzical faces, Mr Spooner smiles and adds, "The balloons are moving because they float through the air.

And they're moving because the poetry cards attached to them are emotional. You see?" He looks around. "Now I want you to feel inspired by what the other children have achieved. I want you all to spend much longer than seven seconds thinking about what you're writing about. So crack on today and write me an emotional poem about an animal. This is where you let your imagination run free."

Lee says his imagination has run so free it's run off.

Ignoring him, Mr Spooner says, "You can write about any animal you want, be it a lion or a bear…" He pauses and looks at Lee. "Or maybe it could be a sloth. Or perhaps you have a pet you can write about. But before you put pens to paper, let me remind you that I'd rather you didn't describe the pet on the outside. I want you to imagine and think about the animal in a deeper way."

"Can I do a spider, sir?" asks Lee. "After Mum's sucked it up with a vacuum?"

"Why on earth would you write about that?"

"Because it must be like being in a cyclone," says Lee. When Mr Spooner asks if Lee even knows what it's like to be in a cyclone, he replies, "Yes, sir, they've got one down the precinct."

Annoyed, Mr Spooner tells Lee that if he wants to write about a spider he can, but the spider must not be in a vacuum as that's not particularly spider-friendly...

"Or on the bottom of a shoe?" Lee asks, hopefully.

Mr Spooner tells Lee he'd prefer the spider to be alive. Then he says, "You can do a spider, but to really get under the skin of what your spider sees and feels, you'll have to write your poem eight times. They have eight eyes, you know."

That shuts Lee up.

I decide to write about Jupiter, because at least that will be easy, although I'm not sure I want to get inside his mind. Not when it's the mind of a killer. I glance over at Dolly-Rose, who is drawing a huge black blob. Her pen is scratching the paper so hard she's almost tearing a hole in it.

"Ah, Dolly-Rose," says Mr Spooner, as he walks past her. "Is this a black...um...woolly sheep? Rather than drawing, I'd prefer you to write a poem. Try your dog or cat or something. Have you got a pet?" he suggests helpfully, but Dolly-Rose shakes her head. Mr Spooner sails past to look at Lee's work and suggests he actually gets a pen out because he won't be able to write without one. Lee says he's writing in invisible ink about a transparent jellyfish. Mr Spooner says he'll be giving him an invisible mark on his school report then.

"I *was* drawing the dog – the black dog," whispers

Dolly-Rose under her breath. When she glances over and realizes I've heard her, she puts her hand over her work and turns away.

"Dolly-Rose's Black Dog"

by Mabel Mynt

It was small and black and had fur
It was a black dog that's for sure
But Dolly-Rose said not at all
She had no pets, big or small
And then she got mad
But her face was all sad
And each time I asked something more
She'd get cross or look to the floor
Or stick SHUT UP right under my nose
I don't understand Dolly-Rose

THE CONSTELLATION
LIGHT

"I was sure there was more money in here," says Mum as I throw my school bag down on the hallway floor. She's staring into her purse and then snaps it shut, muttering that maybe she spent it without realizing when she went out earlier this morning. She doesn't mention the word *appointment*, but I know that's what she meant. After a quick kiss on the cheek, she tells me she's nipping to Bread Pitt for a loaf but she'll be back in fifteen minutes. "And I know I texted you earlier about Topaz not picking you up from school because she had to go to homework club urgently, but what I didn't text is that Gavin is here and he's in the kitchen waiting for you," says Mum, pulling on her coat.

"Why? What for?"

"You'll have to go in and see," answers Mum. "I'll be back soon. Have fun." She closes the front door behind her as I mooch into the kitchen.

Gavin is at the table and he pulls out a chair and tells me to take a seat. He sets an aluminium sheet, scissors, a metal skewer-type object and an empty pickle jar in front of me and goes all mysterious when I ask if we're having pickles on skewers for dinner.

Without another word, Gavin unscrews the lid of the jar and goes to rinse it out in the sink, then dries it with a tea towel before sitting back down. "We don't want the place to stink of onions," he says and gives me a wink.

I just stare. In fact, I might be overcome by pickled onion fumes. As soon as Gavin has peeled the label off the jar, he takes the aluminium sheet and starts cutting it down. All the while he doesn't say a word. I watch as he checks that the sheet fits inside the jar, then he asks if I've guessed what it is yet.

"I don't know!" I yell. Jupiter appears in the kitchen and jumps on the table to have a look. I shoo him away, explaining that he likes to be involved in everything. Jupiter, fuming that he's *not* involved in everything, begins miaowing until I let him out into the garden.

He trots down the path towards the shed and begins scratching at the ground.

Leaving the back door ajar, I come back to the table.

Gavin says, "All right, I'll tell you. I don't want to keep you in suspense." It turns out we're going to make a constellation light. "They're the best because they project a map of the stars onto your wall. I thought you might like it. I picked up some of the bits yesterday when I had a day off."

It's a brilliant idea and I've always wanted the stars on my wall! But then I remember that yesterday Blonde Ponytail Woman seemed to be moving into Gavin's house and it doesn't feel right to be thinking of constellation lights.

"I can't do this," I whisper, shaking my head. I can't get too close to Gavin. Topaz said it – Mum's heart will be broken by him and maybe mine will be too. I pop that worry into the suitcase along with all the others. And then I think about how I'm on my own with the suitcase and how I can't tell Gavin what I'm thinking because I can't expect anyone to understand.

Gavin nudges the jar towards me, saying, "Of course you can. I'm here to help you. Honestly, it's not difficult. And where would we be if we didn't have friends to help us?"

"We're friends?"

"I'd like to think so," says Galactic Gavin and a half smile plays on his lips. "At least, I'm your friend if you want me to be."

I shrug.

"Well, friends or not, would you like to help me make this? Because I've always wanted to make one. You'd be doing me a favour." Gavin clears his throat and takes the aluminium sheet out of the jar and hands it to me. "That's the perfect fit."

"I'd like to make a constellation light too," I say cautiously. "And I guess it wouldn't hurt to be sort of friends. Today, at school, I wanted to be friends with a girl in my class called Dolly-Rose. I even made up a poem about her on the walk home from school. I didn't have Topaz complaining in my ear like she usually does so I had time to do it."

"I bet this Dolly-Rose was pleased you were so friendly."

"She wasn't," I reply, shaking my head. "She told me to shut up."

"Oh."

"But I'd like to be her friend," I add. "I think she looks a bit sad and I imagine it's because she's new and worried about it. She has a dog, even though she said she didn't have a pet. I asked what the dog's name was, but she didn't tell me. I overheard her calling it black dog, so I think that must be what she calls it. I don't think she likes it much."

Gavin pauses, thinks for a second and then replies, "That's an unusual name for a pet. I wonder, if she gave it a nice name like Fluffy, would she like it more?"

I think Gavin has a point.

"I bet you can't imagine calling Jupiter anything else but Jupiter."

I think about what Gavin's said and try to shake away the image of Mum calling Jupiter "THAT FLAMING MOUSE-KILLER." But Gavin's right, maybe Dolly-Rose should try a nice friendly name for her pet. I smile because I have a plan, thanks to Gavin, and I bet when I next speak to Dolly-Rose she doesn't tell me to shut up.

"Shall we finish this little beauty?" Gavin grins and tells me that this constellation light is special because it'll bring the stars into my bedroom and even when I'm feeling down, I can look up.

Instantly, I feel a swell of emotion gallop up my throat. And it's like a cloud has passed over the full moon and everything has turned dark. Gavin looks at me and squeezes my arm and tells me we're doing this together, right? He pulls a sheet of paper printed with constellations on it out of his pocket and says I can put holes in the aluminium sheet with the skewer to correspond to the stars on the paper. Sort of like tracing their pattern. Then we're going to put a battery-operated candle inside. "No real candles," warns Gavin, wagging his finger. "I wouldn't want you to burn the house down."

As I take the paper, I say, "Do you have a house, Gavin?" To be fair, I already know the answer.

Gavin watches as I try to puncture holes in the aluminium sheet using the skewer and says, "Yes, I do."

"Would you ever share your house with someone you love?" I swallow because I already know the answer to this too.

"Of course I would," replies Galactic Gavin, helping me make the holes. "People do that all the time."

My tummy feels like there's a goldfish inside it chasing its tail when I think of Gavin living with Blonde Ponytail Woman. "Do people ever let you down?"

Gavin shrugs and says not everyone is perfect and we can't expect them to be, any more than we should expect ourselves to be perfect. "We're only human. Wouldn't it be nice to stop beating ourselves up about stuff? To be kind to ourselves, just as we're kind to others?"

Gavin is right, we shouldn't beat ourselves up about things. We should be kind to ourselves. But I can't stop the worries building up, or my stomach feeling like it's full of fish swishing around. As I watch Gavin puncture a hole in the aluminium, I say he must be very busy working at the estate agency and visiting his mum. Gavin smiles and says I don't know the half of it, and that makes me think that I probably don't. The other half might be lies – that's what Topaz says. She also told me that Gavin was living a double life and I thought that sounded tricky because living just one life is hard enough.

"Yes, I've got a lot on my plate. And I'm stretching myself thin. Sometimes I feel like I need to be in two places at once," Gavin adds.

"Like you've got a double life?"

"Sort of." Gavin grins.

I feel my heart stutter.

P. C. WHEELER

I don't like the sound of a "sort of" double life. And I think Gavin senses it, because he leans over towards me and whispers, "Life gets complicated and you've got to go with the flow sometimes. Do you understand what I'm trying to say?"

"I d-d-don't want things to change," I stammer, staring at the punctured aluminium sheet. "I'm not sure I like going with the flow either. I'm not sure what I like."

Gavin takes a long breath and plays with his fingers. "Standing still?" He glances at me, then his gaze falls on the half-finished light again. "It's not really an option though, is it? Things can't always stay the same. Not even the stars can do that. Some of them are born and appear to twinkle for the longest time before dying."

I tell him that when things change it is worrying. He looks into my eyes and in that second, I know he understands. Gavin opens his mouth to tell me something else but he stops. I think of the worry suitcase again and I want to tell Gavin about it but gulp down the words. Gavin, sensing I'm struggling, fills the silence by saying, "Yes, change can be worrying. No one knows that more than me. But I also believe it can bring new opportunities with it. Make you view the world differently. Don't you think?"

I concentrate on making tiny holes in the aluminium again.

"Okay, if we imagine life as a journey, then when things don't go in the right direction we've got to say to ourselves, 'Hey, maybe this direction is equally nice' or 'it might get me there quicker' or 'maybe it's slower but I like looking around'." Gavin laughs and says he's probably talking a load of nonsense and I should ignore his pearls of wisdom. "My mum was better at that. Full of wisdom and so clever."

I realize something. "You said 'was'," I manage slowly. "Has your mum died?" For a second, I wonder if it's even worse than Topaz suggested – that Gavin's mum isn't alive and *every time* he says he's with her, he's with Blonde Ponytail Woman instead.

Two circles of red appear on Gavin's cheeks. "No, no. I didn't mean to say that at all. It was a silly mistake. I'm sorry, it was a slip of the tongue. You already know I see Mum every Tuesday afternoon. I wouldn't tell fibs about that." Then Gavin swiftly changes the subject, saying that the constellation light is coming along brilliantly and I'm very good at making things, and I feel a flush of pride from his compliment that I'm sure I'm not supposed to feel. And if Topaz was here she'd be angry and say that I was getting to like Gavin too much and treating him like a dad. Gavin takes the punctured aluminium sheet and wraps it around the inside of the jar and you can see the tiny holes we've made in it. Then he switches on the battery-powered candle and places it inside the jar. "Let's try it out."

"I've got blackout curtains in my room," I offer. Gavin tells me that would be perfect, and we carry the jar upstairs and pull the curtains. The room darkens and then is suddenly illuminated with dozens of tiny pinpricks of light. It looks magical and there are stars on the walls and I stand beside Gavin and tell him it's incredible and thank him for making it for me.

"No, we did it together," corrects Gavin. "Teamwork. Sometimes it's nice to share, and not do everything by yourself."

As I pull the curtains open again, I feel in my heart that I want to show Gavin my *I Need Space* book but my head isn't so sure. I couldn't bring myself to talk about the book in class and I don't know if I can do it now. I pause for a moment and Gavin asks me what I'm thinking about. "Um..." I hesitate, not sure if I should go on, but Gavin smiles, and I whisper that I've got something special I was thinking about sharing with him. Gavin nods and says he'd like that so much and I wander over to my bookcase and carefully take down the book. The milkshake stain is still on the front. The pages are still folded down.

"I love this book so much," I whisper, feeling a lump lodge itself in my throat.

"And you want to share it with me?"

I nod and tell Gavin how it's the best book ever written about the night skies. And I tell him how I wrote to the author once and asked what an astronomer's favourite sweet was. I mention that the publisher wrote back and told me it was fudge and I hold up the book so Gavin can get a closer look. He starts, and I feel pleased that he's as amazed by the book as me.

"I even asked what the author's favourite telescope was. You'll never guess what?"

Gavin mutters, "Was it a SKYVIEWER 2020?"

I grin and my head bobs up and down like a hook-a-duck in a fair. "It was and I'd love one but they're old and you can't get hold of them these days." I pass the book to Gavin and say the author is called Mr P. C. Wheeler. "That's his full title."

Gavin's eyes widen and I feel that he's impressed by my book because he stutters for a second, finding it hard to get the words out. "Mr P. C. Wheeler?"

"Yes."

"Um...right. Do you know anything about P. C. Wheeler?" Gavin's words slink out of his mouth, like a long slow millipede. He flicks the pages back and forth.

I pause and think for a second. "I think he's young and clever and he knows everything and he's the best." Gavin goes to say something but I continue, "He makes the stars come alive with his stories, just like my dad did with his stories about things…" The words disappear on my lips. "I think P. C. Wheeler is brilliant. I just wish this was a signed copy. That would make it even more perfect."

Gavin tells me that it's an incredible book and I offer to let him borrow it but he resists, saying that it's special to me, but he thanks me for sharing it with him. "And I do love the stars too. My mum got me interested in them," he half-whispers.

"My dad sort of got me interested," I offer back. "This was a book he brought home and gave me. That's why it's special." I can't believe I'm talking to Gavin about Dad. I want to say that when Dad left the world tipped upside down and I want to say that I'm happy that Gavin turned up because it made the upside-down world feel a bit better. Gavin tells me that if my dad gave it to me then the book is even more precious, and before I know what I'm doing I give him a hug. It's because of the constellation jar, the chat, for helping me feel like I don't have any worries, just for a second, and for reminding me of how important my book is because it's from Dad. And it doesn't feel awkward or anything and Gavin hugs me right back and then he laughs and says I'm not to squeeze him too hard as he had to eat an awful lot of pickles to get me that jar.

"The Constellation Jar"

by Mabel Mynt

Sometimes there is a little light
That takes away the dark
It gives your life a sense of bright
And glows within your heart

And for one second, for one day
It cleans the dirt like soap
And shines like sunshine's brightest ray
And leaves a sense of hope

I have a jar, it stays with me
And when I'm feeling sad
I watch it and my heart feels free
And suddenly I'm glad

And for one second, for one day
I know that Gav's a star
Thank you for this gift, I say
My constellation jar

TOPAZ'S
GOLDEN HEARTS

Terrible Topaz looks surprised when I knock on her bedroom door and then enter without waiting for a response. She's not long back from homework club, but she went straight to her bedroom without dinner and didn't come out.

Topaz looks up. "What do you want? I haven't called a meeting of the Gavin-is-a-Cheater Club."

I want to tell her that I know there's no meeting but I've had the best time this afternoon and my jaw aches from smiling, but instead I manage, "Gavin is nice, I don't think he's a cheater. He helped me make a constellation light before you got home. You don't do things like that if you're a horrible person. Come downstairs and try to speak to him."

"A what?" There's an edge to Topaz's voice.

"A horrible person."

"Not that bit," replies Topaz.

"Oh. He helped me make a constellation light. It's a jar that throws stars onto the wall when it's switched on. We talked about everything too..." The words trail off as I sense that Topaz's fury is building like a Jenga tower about to topple.

Topaz gets up from the bed and starts pacing up and down. She points to the romance book on her dressing table. "Have you forgotten the love triangle situation already? Can't you see that's what's happening to us?" Topaz puts a finger to the crease of her lips.

"No."

"He's infiltrating this family, Mabel. You're getting to like him." When I say "infiltrating" is a big word, Topaz says she got it from the book she's reading.

"I'm not getting to like him," I reply, my breath catching in my throat. I want to say the truth is *I already like him,* but I can't. I can't say what is inside my heart for fear of making Topaz as furious as a bee caught in a jam jar.

Sometimes when Topaz is in a mood it makes me feel

like I shouldn't get on with Gavin because I'd be betraying Dad or her – that if I get close to Gavin I'm forgetting Dad. I'm not forgetting Dad, but he isn't here. And Gavin is, and he's kind and good to Mum, from what I've seen with my own eyeballs.

Terrible Topaz flicks her hair back and I see something glinting.

"Your ears!" I shriek. "They weren't like that this morning."

"Keep it down. I got them pierced this afternoon," whispers Topaz.

"At homework club?"

"Don't be stupid, I wouldn't let my teachers anywhere near my ears. I wasn't at homework club. And don't tell Mum. I'm going to have to wear my hair down for a while."

"A while?" I stare at Topaz's ears, my eyes goggling at the sight. I quickly add, "You're going to have to wear your hair down for ever, because you're not going to be able to hide those. Mum is going to be cross. She said she was going to take you when she got the chance." Topaz informs me she got them done in the precinct and she had to pretend she was a few years older otherwise they wouldn't do them. "But why did you get them done when you were going to go with Mum?"

Topaz's cheeks flush and she tells me she needed them done sooner. She didn't have time to wait until Mum was ready. Topaz touches her ear with her finger and winces. "They're beautiful, huh? Everyone at school is going to be so impressed. They're going to be chatting about these for ages. Everyone else has them," she mumbles and she rubs her nose. When I say her earlobes look like two red balloons she says I'm just jealous, and I say I am not jealous and she tells me to shush.

"So, what do you think of them really? They're actually little hearts. Proper gold too." I don't answer. Instead I stare up at the ceiling and chew on the inside of my mouth. When Topaz repeats the question, calling me "Cloth-ears", I reply that she told me to shush so I'm just doing what I was told.

"Well un-shush."

"How did you pay for them?" I ask.

"Shush," says Topaz again.

Later, we're sitting in the living room and Mum is in the kitchen making a cup of tea, when Topaz notices a glint at Gavin's neck. She asks him if he's wearing a necklace. Clearing his throat, Gavin says he is and he tells us it's a special one and he pulls it out and shows it to us. There's a golden disc on it with an engraving. Topaz leans right in to get a good look at it and then leans right back. "It says Carina," she says triumphantly. She gives me the side-eye.

"Yes, that's right," replies Gavin and he doesn't look in the least bit worried about it.

"You admit it," says Topaz, nodding gravely. "Who's Carina? Does she have a necklace too?"

Gavin looks perplexed and his eyes dart between us both. "Mabel knows about Carina."

Topaz's eyes flick towards me. Under her breath I hear her mumbling, "*Carina, Carina, Carina.*"

Gavin urges me to explain to Topaz about Carina. I feel my cheeks flame. Gavin holds up his hands and says I don't need to worry about it and if I want he'll explain everything.

I nod, mute.

"Carina is a constellation," he tells Topaz. "Mabel knows all about constellations, don't you? I bet you know all about Carina."

It feels like all the tension in the room has deflated like a bouncy castle going down after a party. Topaz's eyes glaze over as he discusses how Carina is in the southern sky and its name is Latin for the keel of a ship and it was part of a larger constellation called—

"Argo Navis," I say hopefully.

Gavin grins. "Exactly…until it divided into three. So, there was Carina, Puppis and Vela. Did you know that Carina holds one of the brightest stars in the sky, Canopus? I think Carina is pretty special and that's why it's on my necklace."

Terrible Topaz is speechless for once.

"I didn't believe him," blurts out Topaz the next morning at breakfast, adding, "he looked uncomfortable. Shifty, almost. There was more to that necklace than he said and I swear Gavin and Blonde Ponytail Woman have got matching necklaces. That happened in my book."

"Right," I say.

"Those matchy-matchy necklaces are actual love tokens. Signs of affection. You only get them if you're in love." Topaz bites on her lip.

"We don't know if Blonde Ponytail Woman has a matching necklace though."

"Oh, I'm convinced she does," replies Topaz. "And, by the way, did the goblet crack yesterday when Gavin mentioned that Carina was a constellation?"

"Carina *is* a constellation, so it wouldn't have cracked."

"Yes, but I'm sure it's Blonde Ponytail Woman's name too," hisses Topaz. "I bet she's called Carina."

I'm about to shake my head and argue that the goblet didn't crack when Mum appears at the kitchen door. She's looking in her purse again and frowning, mumbling that she could have sworn she had a note in here yesterday and she still doesn't know what she spent it on. "Honestly, I don't know where the money goes these days. It's like I put it in my purse and then it flies away on the breeze." Mum shakes her head.

"Like the seeds of a dandelion clock," whispers Topaz, quickly rising from the table and pulling her hair over her ears.

THE LIBRARY

On Monday morning, Mr Spooner tells us he's decided it would be nice if our parents came to watch our poetry balloons fly away. We'll have a little ceremony, he informs us, and he'll email the information to our parents or guardians. After that he tells us to line up.

"To make sure we're all on top form for our project and that we impress our family and friends, we're going to the school library to study other poets who have gone before us," Mr Spooner explains. "I feel it's important to read poetry, as well as write it."

I'm thinking about how my dad won't come to watch my balloon fly away. I couldn't ask him, even if I wanted to. I close my eyes, trying to imagine Dad clapping as my helium balloon flies into a blue sky; as it bobs beyond the clouds, delivering an emotional poem where each and every word has poured from my heart.

Dolly-Rose interrupts my thoughts by telling me her house in Buckingham Place has a big library, possibly the biggest in Dóchas. She also says that her mother is a part-time poet and writes when she's not carrying out brain surgery and that means that Dolly-Rose is bound to have the writing gene and will probably write a poem that blows Mr Spooner's socks off. To be fair, I'm not sure blowing his socks off is that brilliant an idea. Dolly-Rose is waffling on and on and Mr Spooner, exasperated, is telling us to keep the chit-chat to a minimum. I'm not sure what the maximum chit-chat level is, but I'm pretty sure we're exceeding it. A minute later we're at the school library and Mr Spooner opens the door and ushers us inside, saying, "Welcome to the portal."

"A portal?" Lee's eyes widen. "Like in sci-fi, sir? Are we going through a portal to another time and dimension?" He's so excited he can hardly stand still.

Mr Spooner looks pleased and replies, "Well, that's a good way of putting it, yes."

Lee asks where the portal is exactly because he

wants to go back to the time of the dinosaurs.

"Um...Lee, I think you're taking this a little more literally than I anticipated. The *library* is the portal. You can read about all sorts of places in the world, past, present and future. I'm sure there's a book on dinosaurs here that'll transport you to their time."

"Oh." Lee doesn't look impressed.

Mr Spooner takes us into the far corner of the library and makes us sit down at the tables dotted around the room. He says we're here to discuss some great poets that have gone before us, like Percy—

"Pig!" shouts Lee.

"Bysshe Shelley," says Mr Spooner, tapping the desk with his finger. "And wordsmiths like Wordsworth. Class, please take this opportunity to acquaint yourself with these poets and many others. We have a section here on poetry and I'd like you to use it. There are poets of the past and poets of the present and hopefully I've got a few poets of the future here in front of me. Right, scoot. Look around the library, look for poems that inspire you."

We all scoot.

Except Lee.

Mr Spooner stares at him then shouts that we're supposed to be working, not lounging around like we'd do in our living room. Lee doesn't notice because he has just face-planted in a beanbag.

Meanwhile, half the class are chatting and the other half are looking at books. I scan the shelves and spot a book that looks familiar, called *Daydreaming Daisy*. I take it from the shelf and idly read the back. Apparently, it's about a girl whose father is a scientist and her mum a... I'm just trying to find out more when Dolly-Rose grabs it from my hand and shoves it back on the shelf, saying her living room is much bigger than this library. From behind us Mr Spooner pops up, reminding us again that we need to work. We're here to pick and study some poems and we can choose anything, whether they're happy poems or sad ones. "Some poets you will connect with and those are the poets to study in more depth, so you can look beneath the surface and interpret their words."

Dolly-Rose says, "I don't like sad poems because I'm never sad." When I say everyone is a bit sad sometimes, she tells me that her life is perfect.

The thing is, if it's so perfect, why does she look sad right now?

I'm about to ask that very question when Lee jumps up from the beanbag and starts talking loudly in his friend's ear. Meanwhile, Mr Spooner is getting more cheesed off than melted cheese on a four-cheese pizza with cheesy stuffed crust, and telling us that he can hear a lot of chatter and if we don't behave he'll take us back to the classroom. Lee says this sounds good and then Mr Spooner informs us that when we get back to the classroom he can give us extra maths. Lee says this doesn't sound good.

Then Mr Spooner beckons us over and says we're to huddle around because he has some news, but we have to be quiet and listen because he couldn't bring his maracas into the library. "You need to be silent in here," he says. Which is daft because Mr Spooner is the only one talking now. "I've decided the best poem in this project will win some sweets. I think that's a nice gesture for all your hard work. Maybe mints. What could be better than that?"

"Chocolate," offers Lee.

While Mr Spooner is giving Lee a firm talking-to about going in his Bad Books and Lee is asking if the Bad Books are in the library, Dolly-Rose has wandered off and picked up a book with a dog on the front. At first, I'm not sure if I should, but right now I'm certain this is the time to put my plan into action. I came up with it when Gavin and I were making the constellation light and the more I think about it the more I'm convinced it'll make Dolly-Rose smile and we'll be best friends. I take a piece of paper and quickly scribble: EBONY, MIDNIGHT, ASH, BEETLE, LIQUORICE, POPPY, INK, RAVEN, SMUDGE, SOOT and pass it to Dolly-Rose and I whisper that maybe she should give her black dog a nice name. "This might cheer you up. I mean, you look a bit sad and maybe it's because of your dog. You can't call it Black Dog," I hiss. "I've given you a few suggestions." I feel quite smug, I'm not going to lie.

Dolly-Rose gives me a few words of suggestion back. They include: DON'T SHUT I'LL IN THE SHINS IF YOU UP KICK YOU (not necessarily in that order). The rest of her suggestions I don't care to repeat at all. Clearly, Gavin's idea of naming the dog something like Fluffy was as much use as a chocolate hot-water bottle in the Sahara.

At midday, when we've finished reading the poetry books and discussing our favourites, Mr Spooner says it's time to go back to the classroom. He swings open the library door and we all spill out and march down the corridors, keeping in line. I sidle up to Dolly-Rose, making sure my shins aren't anywhere near her feet, and I say I'm sorry that I tried to give her suggestions for her dog's name. I understand that she'd rather name it herself. I tell Dolly-Rose I'm interested in her life and family, but only because I want to be her friend and it's easy to feel nervous or worried when you start something new, like Nana Anna says, but I'd be a good friend. Dolly-Rose grunts and says she doesn't care what Nana Anna says because she's not worried and doesn't need a friend. To be honest, I thought everyone needed a friend sometimes.

"Okay, I could tell you about my life instead," I offer, trying to keep the conversation going. Nana Anna says it's nice to strike up a conversation and even if the other people don't try, you should. Dolly-Rose sticks her nose in the air as if she's not interested in my boring life. I quickly move onto the subject of stars and I tell Dolly-Rose how much I love them. I tell her how there are at least one hundred billion galaxies in the universe and how a starburst galaxy is a galaxy that forms stars at a fast rate.

"I thought Starbursts were sweets," says Dolly-Rose. "Who taught you about the stars anyway?"

"A book mainly. And I talk about them with..." I swallow. For a second the words feel stuck, but then they tumble out: "Gavin. He's nice. He knows that the footprints the astronauts left on the moon are still there. And he knows that if there was a bathtub big enough to hold it, Saturn would float. And it's windy on Uranus."

I find myself smiling, which is better than how I felt a few seconds ago.

For the first time since I've met her, Dolly-Rose smiles too.

THE SURPRISE

"Why don't you walk home with your friends?" I mumble when I spy Terrible Topaz at the school gate. "You don't need to meet me every day, you know. I'm not a baby."

Topaz pauses and knocks my head with her knuckles, like it's a front door. "Hello, I had to come here today because we're meeting Mum, remember?" Topaz is right, because Mum told us this morning she was taking us to town. Okay, that explains today, but not every other day.

I flip my school bag over my shoulder and as we head towards the end of the street where all the cars are parked, I tell Topaz that we're going to write our poems for the Poetry in (e)Motion project on a piece of card and then we're attaching the card onto a balloon.

"Balloon?" Topaz stares at me.

"Yes," I reply.

"But why bother?"

"Why not?" I blink, thinking Topaz's question is stupid. "It's fun. We're all doing it. I bet you and your friends do projects like that at school all the time. It's no big deal."

Topaz's eyes flick to the pavement. The smile drops from her lips and she twists her fingers, squeaking something about us not discussing her bazillions of friends. This is not about them. "I don't care what you do anyway," Topaz says with a shrug, marching ahead. "I don't care about anything."

That's a lie, because she cares about what Gavin's doing to Mum. As Topaz hurries in front of me, I see a flash of purple in her hair.

"Topaz, you've got paint in your hair," I yell.

When I catch up with her, Topaz says it's not paint. "It's a strand of faux hair that you clip in. It's fashion."

"It's fake," I mutter.

Topaz says all the girls in her class are doing it.

"But it looks weird. And where did you get it?"

Topaz tells me she paid for it, like she paid to get her ears pierced. I'm about to ask how (because Mum only gives us money when we clean our bedrooms and considering the mess Topaz's room is in, I doubt Mum gave her a penny) when we hear Mum's car horn tooting.

Mum waves and beckons us into the car. "Hiya, you two," she says as we climb in. "Let's nip to town and get some bits for the house."

"Why?" Topaz asks.

Mum swings the car left at a junction. "I thought it might be nice to get some photo frames and change the house around a little bit. It's been the same since..." I know Mum's about to say "since your dad left" but she doesn't because she can't seem to talk about Dad without looking sad. Instead she says, "Since for ever. And now Gavin's coming around a lot more, I thought we could add a few things – perhaps a few pictures, maybe even include him in some of them? I promise I won't change everything but maybe a few things. Make him feel welcome – like he's part of the family." Mum turns the steering wheel.

"Did Galactic Gavin make you do this?" says Topaz, tossing back her hair. I catch sight of the purple streak again.

"No," replies Mum, keeping her eyes fixed on the road. "And why are you calling him Galactic Gavin, Topaz?"

Under her breath, Topaz mutters, "Cause he's from another planet and it's a planet I don't like."

"It's Gavin or even Gav," continues Mum. "Anyway, I just thought it would be nice, now he's in our lives. The odd photo wouldn't hurt. You wouldn't object to that, would you?"

I know Topaz *does* object, but she doesn't say so. Instead I can see she's furiously bubbling inside, like a volcano about to erupt.

Condensation builds on the inside of the car window and I draw a tiny balloon shape with my fingertip. Changing the subject, because Topaz has a face like thunder, I tell Mum that we're doing a poetry project at school, writing poems and tying them on balloons before letting them go.

"Parents can come along and hear us read the work and watch the balloons float up to the sky…" I hesitate and stare at the little balloon I've drawn on the window. Then the words tumble out. "Mr Spooner is going to email you. Mums and dads can come." I pause. "I bet Dad would love it." The words hang in the air like tiny droplets of water hanging from a leaf after the rain.

Mum takes the second exit at the roundabout. "Oh, that's a clever idea. I'm sure the balloons will look spectacular floating away on the breeze. I'll be there and perhaps Gavin too, if that's okay with you." That's all she says. She doesn't mention Dad.

Topaz lets out a snort.

No Dad, no chance to ask him, no nothing. This is not going well. I don't even know why I mentioned Dad. No one ever talks about him these days. My throat burns and I feel tears prickle my eyes, but I blink to make them disappear. I haven't forgotten Dad – how could I when I've still got the space in my heart?

I swipe my hand over the balloon drawing on the glass and it disappears, like Dad did. There's nothing left except tiny rivers of water like teardrops running down the window. Meanwhile, Topaz is trying to hide the heart earrings in her ears by covering them with hair (that isn't purple), Mum is staring straight ahead, and I'm in the back, stuffing more and more worries in my suitcase. I'm sure the suitcase is full, certain that it's not going to be possible to add more. And then I remind myself that there's always room for one more worry. Always...

"Can you two stop moping around?" asks Mum, swinging the car into a parking space five minutes later.

"There's plenty of time for that when you've got a mortgage and a couple of pre-teens to look after, like me." She turns off the engine, ushers us out of the car and locks it, and we all troop towards the shops.

We haven't even reached them before Topaz pipes up with a question. "What would happen if a man was cheating?" Topaz lets it sink in before adding, "I mean, what would you even do if it was Gavin. Just asking um...for a friend."

I nearly faint in shock. Stranger still, Mum laughs.

"Imagine that!" Mum replies. Topaz is about to say we don't have to imagine it when Mum continues, "Gavin wouldn't have time to cheat. He works too hard to have the chance to see anyone else. You're reading too many romance books – they're fiction, Topaz. Those books are made up. You're imagining things."

With that, Mum swishes into the shop and starts picking up photo frames, chuckling to herself as if Terrible Topaz has told her the funniest joke. She says that she'd love to have a photo of Gavin on the bookcase in the living room. I shrug and Topaz rolls her eyes so hard it's a wonder they don't fall out of their sockets and speed down the aisles.

When Mum's not in earshot, Topaz leans in and says, "She thinks I'm imagining it. But I'm not and I'm going to prove it. Let's try to get that Goblet of Truth to work one more time."

Mum stops in front of a noticeboard and she's looking at little business cards and says she's thinking of getting the bathroom tiles redone. Plucking a card from the board, Mum pops it in her pocket and says there's a local woman who can do the job. We trail around after Mum as she picks up bits and pieces and after a while Topaz is so bored she nearly falls asleep on a chair in the furniture department. When she starts drooling, Mum nudges her and tells her there's no time to snooze because she's just remembered she needs to get light bulbs.

"I'm not sure where they are," mumbles Mum, her eyes searching from right to left across the store. That's when Mum spies someone with their back to us, who's wearing an orange jacket with the words HERE TO HELP on the back. "Excuse me," says Mum, tapping the woman on the shoulder. "Where are your light bulbs?"

The woman turns around and Topaz's eyes are like two boiled eggs and her mouth drops open into a giant hula hoop of horror. The woman smiles and flicks her blonde ponytail over her shoulder. She tells Mum that the bulbs are at the far end and she can show us exactly where.

"No, no," replies Mum, smiling back. "Honestly. I can find them myself. You don't want to be running around too much, not in your condition." Mum makes us walk down to the lighting department with her. "I need a forty-watt bulb," she says, scanning the shelves, completely unaware that something apocalyptic has just happened.

"That was Blonde Ponytail Woman, otherwise known as Carina," whispers Topaz, giving me a tiny punch on the arm. She pauses under a giant fluffy light that looks like an angel's wings. Her face is burning with anger.

"I know," I whisper back.

"She works here."

"Yes."

"She's having a baby," hisses Topaz.

"I could see that," I reply.

"It must be Galactic Gavin's."

THE FINAL LIE

When you think things can't get any worse, they do –
a million times worse. Later that evening I wander into
the living room and throw myself on the sofa beside
Mum. She's watching her favourite TV cookery
programme called *The Huge Cake-Off* where they make
things like buns, cakes and fudge and then get judged
on which is best. Mum's perched on the edge of her
seat, saying this sounds like it'll be a good recipe for
sea-salt fudge and it could sell in Fudge Fudge Wink
Wink. I tell Mum sea salt and fudge have no business
being together and Mum laughs and tells me if I applied
that logic we wouldn't have cheese and cake either or

mud and pie. Then she asks me to run and get her little notebook and a pen from her bag in the hall, because she wants to jot down the recipe quickly. I get up and trot into the hallway and, finding Mum's bag, nosy through it like a fox rummaging through a bin.

"Hurry up," shouts Mum. "Or the recipe will be gone."

I pull out a photo and it's one of Mum, Dad and Topaz and me. I didn't know Mum was still carrying it around. I carry things though – so why shouldn't Mum? My fingers touch Dad's face and it feels as though my heart is racing, jumping over hurdles, thundering down a course. I pause, the photo quivering in my hand and remember how it was taken at Dóchas Rock on a sunny day when we had a picnic. My mind drifts back to what Mr Spooner said about pictures having a story behind them. On the surface this is only a photograph, but there's so much more behind it. We sat on a tartan blanket that day and ate triangle-shaped sandwiches and crisps from a tube and Dad pointed out the rock and told Topaz and me how you could stand on it and your worries would float away. Topaz never said much but I know she loved the story, but me, I loved it so much that Dad retold it to me every night at bedtime, just before the fist bump and the "I love you." I didn't have worries then, or if I did they weren't as heavy. Then the sun disappeared soon after and Mum and Dad were arguing and the day ended with a storm.

"What are you doing out there?" yells Mum. "Can't you find it?" I call back that I'll only be a second and I put the photo back but then accidentally pull out a corner of a piece of paper, which looks like an email Mum has printed but torn up afterwards. It mentions a visitor's appointment at 10.30 a.m. last Friday. Only it doesn't say what it was for or where Mum went.

Mum appears in the hallway and snatches the bit of paper from my hand and says I shouldn't be reading that, even though there wasn't much to read. My face burns like the inside of a molten hot apple pie. And I say I wasn't reading it. To be honest, it didn't make much sense anyway. And what's the big secret about this appointment? Why hasn't Mum said where she was going? Annoyed, Mum picks up her bag and takes it into the living room, telling me I shouldn't be snooping. I feel like saying I wasn't snooping because Mum asked me to go into her bag.

But I don't.

The next morning, Topaz peers out of her bedroom door and stops me at the top of the stairs, telling me things are more catastrophic than she thought. She says she didn't see the baby coming.

"Didn't you spot her belly when you first spied her with the ring?" I ask.

Topaz tuts. "She was wearing a coat that looked like a giant duvet the first time I saw her. So, no, I didn't. And then she had a box in front of her stomach when we saw her at Galactic Gavin's house."

I swallow. "We won't have a new brother or sister, will we?"

"Don't be dopey," snaps Topaz, her eyes like flint. "It's got nothing to do with us. I wish the goblet would hurry up and reveal another lie. We've got to tell Mum about Galactic Gavin *before* the baby arrives."

Topaz ducks back into her bedroom and I slink downstairs to the kitchen, dragging the worry suitcase with me.

I'm sitting at the kitchen table, staring at the Goblet of Truth and trying to figure out why Gavin would lie to us, and why he has a necklace saying Carina, and could it be both a woman's name and a constellation, and why the man at the estate agency lied to us too, telling us he knew nothing about Gavin and the ring (when he so obviously did). And that's when something terrible happens. The Goblet of Truth gets to work, just like

Topaz said. Only this time, I discover Mum is lying! And this is the third and final lie. Here's how it happens.

"Why do you keep putting that cup on the table?" asks Mum, bustling into the kitchen and sitting down. She stares at the goblet, pauses, shakes her head and continues, "I'm sure I've seen it somewhere else before. It definitely looks familiar." Mum scratches her cheek. "Nope, it's gone. I can't remember."

For a second, I think about telling Mum what the goblet's all about and how Jupiter brought it in. But I figure she wouldn't be happy if she knew it was a magic cup *and* we were using it to prove Gavin is a liar. No, I don't think Mum would like that at all. Anyway, I swear she's still in a bit of a mood after I said Dad would love my balloon ceremony at school and after I found that torn-up email mentioning an appointment. She pours herself a cup of tea and takes a sip, then rises from the table, wanders into the hall and yells to Topaz to get out of bed. When Topaz doesn't reply, Mum stomps upstairs and she's shouting that school's not going to wait for Miss Topaz Mynt and I hear her say, "You don't seem to want to go to school these mornings. What's the problem?"

There's a pause.

Next, I hear Mum yell, "What on earth is going on

with your ears? Are they pierced? I told you I'd take you. I didn't say you could go on your own. When did you get those done?" There follows a heated conversation and Topaz is yelling back that she had them done a few days ago and wants to be like everyone else in her class. And Mum is squawking that it's okay to be different and Topaz is screaming back that no one wants to be different because that means you're weird and Mum is yelling weird is good.

I lift my spoon to my mouth and chew on a mouthful of cereal, my eyes fixed on the goblet.

Now, Mum's shouting like she wants someone in Australia to hear her and Topaz is shouting back like she wants someone in New Zealand to hear her. Mum yells that she has a school meet-the-head-and-other-parents-in-your-child's-class tomorrow and Topaz has put her in a bad mood that will last at least twenty-four hours. She squeals that it's very silly to go off and get your ears pierced and she didn't get an adult to give permission. Round One to Mum. Topaz shouts that *Mum* must be very silly then because *her* ears are pierced. Round Two to Topaz. Mum points out that Topaz has to look after her ears and if she doesn't, she might get an infection. She also mentions that the school won't like her wearing big earrings if they're doing PE. Round

Three to Mum. Topaz shouts that she will look after her ears and put in lots of lovely new earrings, not big. Round Four to Topaz. Mum shouts who paid for them? Round Five to Mum, and then she delivers the knockout blow that'll she ground Topaz if she doesn't behave herself. Ding ding! Mum is the winner.

While they're yelling, I lift the goblet and just as I'm about to put it in my pocket I hear the letter box rattle. I rise from the chair and go into the hallway and grab a letter from the mat and Mum's shouting at me now, asking if that was the post that just came through the letter box because she's expecting something. "Yeah," I fire back. I take the letter into the kitchen and prop it up against the milk carton. The writing is thin and spidery and I sit on the chair and stare at it:

Mrs Tracey Mynt
22 Bristo Road
Dóchas

My heart stutters inside my ribcage. "Dad?" I whisper. Peering closer at the writing, I can see all the swirls and loops and the funny way he used to cross his "t"s. It's Dad's writing, I know it. My hands tremble as I imagine Dad writing on the envelope and wonder if he's not as far away as I thought and I wish that there's a note inside written to me and it says: *I am sorry I left and never came back. I didn't mean to disappear and I'm coming back now and I'll never do that again. One night you will look out the window and I will walk up the garden path and that heavy suitcase of yours will disappear because I'll be there. Then we'll fist-bump and say, "I love you," just like we used to. And there will no longer be a space in your heart where I used to be.*

"But why did you disappear in the first place?" I whisper, feeling my grip tighten on the goblet. The last time I saw Dad's writing was on a notepad, telling Mum to pick up some milk because he forgot to get it. That was ages ago and the notepad has vanished, just like Dad. "And I want you to come back and I want you to tell me stories about the rock." I pause. "I want you to make it okay. I want you to say you love me and I'll say it in return."

Mum suddenly appears in the kitchen, asking where the post is.

I nod towards the letter, still propped up where I placed it. Mum's cheeks are like two rosy-red apples when she spies it and she snatches up the envelope and starts saying it's not what I think. "It's a bill," says Mum firmly. "It's not important. They'll be looking for more money." I didn't know Mum had X-ray vision. How else would she know what was inside? She hasn't opened it yet. Anyway, don't bills come with little windows so you can see the address? Mum doesn't like envelopes with windows – that's what she told me before.

"But it looks like Dad's writing," I manage. There's a volcano building inside me and my fingers crush against the goblet. I stare at Mum for answers but she doesn't look my way. "What if there's a note inside for me?" The words explode around me like fireworks and my grip tightens on the gold cup.

"It's not and there isn't," says Mum and her jaw hardens.

I nod but my tongue sticks to the roof of my mouth and no words come out. Instead, I realize my hand feels hot and clammy where I'm clutching the goblet. When I release it, I look down and I see a third crack in the cup. One that I didn't notice before. Horrified, I'm not sure if I've cracked the cup under the pressure or if Mum is lying. But the feeling in my gut tells me it's Mum and she's definitely fibbing to me. So now I have another worry to add to the suitcase. I look up, my eyes stinging with tears, and furiously blink them away as Mum casually folds the envelope up and shoves it in her handbag without opening it. Then she takes out her purse, saying, "It's a bill and nothing you need to concern yourself with. Nothing at all. Now, shouldn't you be getting to school? It's bad enough that your sister is upstairs and she secretly got her ears pierced. I don't want any trouble from you too."

And I wonder, why should asking about your dad count as causing trouble?

BONNIE TILER

Mum's gone with Topaz to school this morning for the meet-the-head-and-other-parents-in-your-child's-class coffee morning. So, on the way to school I have no Topaz to bleat in my ear and that means I have extra time to worry about Mum lying.

In fact, I worry all day. I worry so much that I don't eat my sandwiches at lunchtime. I worry in afternoon lessons too. I worry when Mr Spooner tells us a story about the Ancient Greek Hippocrates diagnosing patients by tasting their wee.

I'm still worrying when I'm walking home from school with Topaz. She's telling me about how she's got so many friends at her new school that she can't fit them all on her phone, although she's tried. She says her fingers are sore from typing all the phone numbers into her contacts. I mumble something about it being nice she's so popular, but I'm hardly listening because inside I'm worrying about how everything feels upside down at the moment. When I worry, my head aches, my stomach knots and it feels like a gobstopper has stuck in my throat. Sometimes I swallow so many times it's like my voice box is on a trampoline. Up-down. Up-down. Up-down. But no one notices. The worries are always silent.

We're in our road, about six houses away from home, when Topaz points to a van with the words **BONNIE TILER – WHATEVER THE STYLE, WE'VE GOT THE TILE** on the side. A giant thumbs-up is painted on the side and as we draw closer we can see a small air-freshener shaped like a tree dangling in the front. Dad once bought a load of those to sell. He said they'd make anyone's car smell like a forest. Mum, after sniffing one, said they'd make anyone's car smell like stinky feet.

Topaz is tweaking a friendship bracelet on her wrist as we wander towards our house. When I ask her if one of her millions of friends gave it to her, she replies, "Um...kind of." Changing the subject, she says, "Do you think we're getting a new bathroom then?"

"Maybe Mum's getting a quote for the tiles," I reply, pausing at our gate. "She mentioned it when we went to that shop." The words trail off and I don't say anything else in case Topaz starts ranting about Blonde Ponytail Woman again. But Topaz has already made the same connection between the shop and Blonde Ponytail Woman working there and now she's complaining again about how Gavin is cheating.

I hoist my school bag back up on my shoulder and click open the latch on the gate as Topaz carries on. "Mum doesn't believe Galactic Gavin has time to cheat but he does. We'll show her and then she won't say he's too busy to have another girlfriend. And she won't be able to say my books are all made up."

"They are," I reply.

"I know," says Topaz. "But we're not making this up about Galactic Gavin. And I bet you haven't thought of this – Mum could be decorating because Galactic Gavin's moving in and then he'll be living between Mum and Blonde Ponytail Woman." With that, Topaz pushes past me and trots down the path.

As we reach the front door, it flies open. A woman with long copper-coloured hair appears on the doorstep, wearing a pair of navy-blue overalls with the words

BONNIE TILER embroidered on the chest in bright pink. Mum is there too, saying, "Thank you, Chrissy," and, "That's great," and "I'll be in touch."

"I thought she was called Bonnie," whispers Topaz, as the woman nods at us. She reminds me of someone, only I'm not sure who. She walks down our path and jumps into the van. It roars into life and she zooms off along the road as Mum waves goodbye and then ushers us into the house.

"What's with you two?" asks Mum, watching us throw our school bags down in the hall. "You've both got faces like wet weekends."

"That's Mabel's usual face," says Topaz, kicking off her shoes. She pauses for a second and then asks what Mum's doing with the bathroom and Mum says she's thinking of getting it tiled and it's not a big deal. "Are you doing it for Galactic— I mean Gavin? Is he moving in?"

Mum snorts and says she's not doing that and she's her own independent woman and she can manage to do things by herself, thank you very much. Topaz asks if Mum would be happy without a boyfriend. "Of course I would," says Mum indignantly.

Topaz looks at me, triumph in her eyes. And I know what she's thinking – if we tell Mum the truth about

Blonde Ponytail Woman, Mum will be fine without Gavin. I know Mum would cope, but I still reckon she'd be sad.

"I just thought the bathroom was looking a bit tired. It's not a criminal off..." The words die on Mum's lips and she quickly says, "It's not a big deal," and then goes into the kitchen. I flop down on the living room sofa and pet Jupiter, who is curled up like a black comma on the cushion. He lifts his head and I scratch under his chin. Beyond the door I can hear the sound of pots and pans rattling and Mum calls into the living room, "Oh, the tiling lady said her daughter just started at your school."

"Mine?" shouts Topaz.

"No," Mum bellows back. "Your school, Mabel. She has a girl. Now what was her name? I think she'd be in your class, because Chrissy said she was your age." There's a pause and the sound of gushing water from the tap. "Um...it was Polly-Rae or Molly-Mae or something like that."

For a second, I'm puzzled. "Dolly-Rose?"

"That was it."

But I thought Dolly-Rose's mother was a brain surgeon.

After dinner, the phone rings in the hallway. I always like to be first to get to it but Mum gets there first this time and I hear her say hello. There's a pause that seems to take for ever and then instead of sounding all jolly, like when Nana Anna rings, Mum sounds serious. "Why are you ringing me at home? Anyone could have picked up the phone. I thought we agreed you wouldn't ring me at home and I'd come in again. We make appointments. You can't change the rules."

There's a pause.

"No."

Silence.

"No. No."

Silence.

I find myself sitting on the stairs, just like I did when Mum threw the books down the hallway. I remember that evening, when Dad left, and how it made me feel. A tiny part of me feels the same way now and I don't know why. I rest my head against the rose wallpaper.

"No."

I inhale then hold my breath, waiting for Mum to say something different.

"No."

I exhale again, defeated.

Mum hisses, "I am not happy with this."

On the night Dad left, Mum said those exact words. I remember feeling a ripple of shock thread down my spine. I'd never heard Mum say she wasn't happy before. And I didn't want my mum to be unhappy. I listen again as Mum says she can't do this until everything is sorted out. She won't be rushed into things and this will all take time.

"Haven't we been through enough? I'm doing what's best and at a slow pace. We don't want to rush things... Yes, I know."

My foot has decided to nod off and I flap it around like a seal's flipper as I ask myself who Mum can be talking to. It's not Nana Anna because Mum always shouts down the phone when it's her because Nana Anna can't hear properly. I'm worrying so much it makes it hard to breathe and my eyes are stinging. None of this makes any sense – nothing does. This is another Mum worry on top of the worry about the envelope that looked like it was written by Dad but Mum said it wasn't. I never thought Mum would lie about anything, not to me. I stare at the roses on the wallpaper, my eyes suddenly blurred by forming tears. I run my finger along the stem of a rose, touching each thorn, before I wipe away a tiny river of water on my cheek and then rise from the stairs.

Later that night, I'm in my bedroom curled up like a Quaver when Mum appears at the bedroom door and says, "Hey."

"Hey," I echo.

Mum comes in and sits down on the bed beside me and strokes my hair. "It's late. Shouldn't you be getting some sleep?"

"Who was on the phone?" I ask.

"A friend," replies Mum, not meeting my eyes. Her eyelids drop and she rubs her nose, saying it was nothing important and I shouldn't be listening to her conversations.

I swallow and then whisper, "I wasn't. But aren't friends important?" Mum says of course they are. A second later my mouth surprises me by saying, "I don't like lies."

Startled, Mum replies, "Well, yes, no one does, but I imagine we probably all tell the odd little white lie. Sometimes we do it so as not to hurt someone's feelings."

"But what if you hurt their feelings anyway?"

Mum snuggles the duvet up around me. "Why are you even mentioning it? Is this about the phone call or the letter? I told you the phone call was a friend and the letter was a bill. Is something else troubling you,

Mabel?" I shake my head and it feels like I've got a carousel spinning around in my belly. Mum explains, "I don't think any of us would deliberately want to hurt someone, now would we? Anyway, I don't want you worrying because it's bedtime and you should be thinking nice thoughts. You don't want to have bad dreams." And with that, the conversation is closed.

When Mum leaves the room, I switch on my constellation light and watch as the pinpricks of light scatter across the walls. After a while, it hurts to look at them so I close my eyes. I want to talk to Mum about my worries so much and explain all the fears inside my head so she understands, but I can't get the words out and the worry suitcase feels so heavy today that my head hurts. I pull the duvet right up and all the worries turn into one big jumble and for a second I don't think I'll ever be able to crawl out from under their weight.

It's ages before I fall asleep and when I do I dream that I'm at the window and I can see down into the street and then I gaze up. Above me the inky sky has been scattered with flecks of white. There are big dots, some tiny, some splash across the heavens, glinting like diamond reflections on a dark sea. And the moon is a pearly crescent, like a lopsided smile on a black blanket. I breathe in and out. But then the worry suitcase arrives and it lands on my shoulders and I'm trying to carry it around but it gets so heavy that I crumble beneath it and then I see a dark figure wandering up the garden path and I open my mouth to call "Dad!" but the words dissolve. I hope he'll help me but I never find out. Because that's when I wake up, sweat running in tiny rivulets through my hair. The constellation light is still on, illuminating the darkness, and although I feel sad that Dad's not here I think of Gavin and the light and I smile and for that moment I feel okay.

"My Life"

by Mabel Mynt

Worry worry worry
BIG worry, small worry
Worry in a hurry
Worry at home
Worry in class
Worry when you're alone

Worry worry worry
BIG worry, small worry
Worry about your mum
Worry about your dad
Worry for your sister
Worry makes me sad

Pack up all your worries
Tell no one what you know
That worries stay inside you
And worries never go...

THE DOLL'S HOUSE

The next day, at school, I draw a picture of a star and then I scribble it out again, because nothing is feeling particularly bright and sparkly in my life at the moment. I try to picture Mum and Gavin together, but I keep getting an image of Blonde Ponytail Woman and her big belly in my head and it won't go away. Mr Spooner strolls past me and says it's an interesting doodle but we're not here to scribble the day away.

"Save your drawings for another time," he insists, wandering back to the front of the class. He blows his nose, then scrunches up the tissue and throws it in the bin. "Okay, I just wanted to let you know that on the day we release the poetry balloons I'd like someone special, perhaps a celebrity or a well-known person, to give us the countdown. Does anyone know someone who could fit the bill?" Mr Spooner's eyes scan the classroom and focus on Dolly-Rose. "Anyone who has a parent with an amazing job like...um...say, a nuclear scientist or a brain surgeon?"

Dolly-Rose pretends to be busy playing with the Velcro strap on her shoe.

"Er, okay, no one then?" Mr Spooner looks disappointed.

Lee puts up his hand. "How about Elvis, sir?"

"Elvis?" Mr Spooner looks confused. "He's dead."

"No, sir. He works in The Frying Squad, near my dad's office in Paradise Precinct. My dad says he sings in the clubs sometimes. But he's not dead because he served us pickled egg and chips last night. He has a big jar of eggs on the counter."

Mr Spooner clears his throat and says he'll give it some more thought. But he gives it no thought, because straight away he says, "Anyone else know someone?" When there's still no answer he adds, "Okay, I'll file that idea away in my head." He taps his forehead and then says, "There's still space for a few more suggestions. But while you're thinking, I'd like you to practise writing a poem on a piece of card and then you can decorate the card too, if you'd like. We haven't tried that yet. Remember to write the poem in the centre and any decoration goes around the outside." Mr Spooner tells us that he's left a kaleidoscope of coloured card, felt tips and glitter on the back table and we can go and choose whatever we want. We could even write our poem like a rainbow, using lots of different colours for the words and then add glitter to that. Be creative, he tells us.

Everyone jumps up from their seats and wanders down to the table at the back to collect card, felt tips and glitter, except Dolly-Rose. So, I pick her a bright pink card and a navy-blue felt tip and some silver glitter, take them to her desk and set them in front of her. She glances up at me and I say, "You need these too."

We're ten minutes into shaking glitter everywhere. And Mr Spooner is ten minutes into shouting until he is hoarse that glitter isn't for fun, which is daft, because it totally is.

Fifteen minutes later, Mr Spooner looks up and says he needs someone to take a message to Mrs Latham in First Class. "Dolly-Rose, can you go?" When Dolly-Rose says she's not sure where the First classroom is, Mr Spooner tells me to go with her and we're both to wait for a reply.

We walk down the corridors in silence and then knock on Mrs Latham's door and a voice shouts, "Come in." The classroom is empty because the little children are outside playing. We can hear them whooping. The classroom looks like how you'd imagine the inside of a rainbow, all bright colours and sparkles. We hand Mrs Latham the note and she opens it and tells us we will need to wait so she can go and get the information and take it back to Mr Spooner. When she leaves the room, we look around at the toys and a large wooden doll's house in the corner.

"Look at this," I say, swinging open the doll's-house door and admiring the grand interior. "I bet your house is like a bigger version of this," I add cautiously.

Dolly-Rose replies, "Much bigger." She peeps inside at all the furniture and little wooden dolls, and she lifts the mother doll from the living room and places her in the bed and tucks her up under a tiny duvet. Then she moves the little girl doll from the playroom and puts her in the chair beside the mother. "She's looking after her," whispers Dolly-Rose, her face dropping like a flipped pancake that didn't quite land in the frying pan. "That's what she does."

"Why isn't she playing instead of looking after the mother?" I peep into all the rooms, one by one.

"She plays a bit," explains Dolly-Rose. "But at other times she tries to look out for her mum. The mum is sad, see. Not just a bit fed up though because most people feel that way sometimes."

I peer into the doll's house and look at the mother doll and she's smiling in bed and I can't see what Dolly-Rose is on about. The doll isn't sad at all. She's lying in bed with a big smile on her face. When I tell Dolly-Rose that the mother doll is happy, she replies that anyone can paint a smile on their face and that doesn't mean anything. Then she leans down and reaches into the kitchen and takes a small black dog that is sitting by the fireplace and places it outside the bedroom door. "He can't come in," says Dolly-Rose fiercely. "I'm stopping him."

"*You?*"

"I mean the girl doll won't let him in. He's not allowed. She's trying to block him by being jolly and doing things. Lots of things." Dolly-Rose pauses and bites her lip. "She's trying to help everyone, but sometimes she doesn't know what to do. Then other people say, 'Snap out of it, love,' or 'Pull yourself together,' to the mum and that isn't the best thing to say."

I watch as Dolly-Rose smooths down the little girl

doll's dress. She sighs. "Anyway, I'm just playing. It's not real."

As the door swings open and Mrs Latham appears with a note, I whisper, "I know it's not real," to Dolly-Rose and she turns away.

On the way back to class I try to ask Dolly-Rose about her mum being a brain surgeon. The truth is, I really want to know if she's a tiler too. But Dolly-Rose doesn't give me any information. Instead she says she can't talk about her mother's job as it's complicated.

"Like brain surgery," I say.

Swiftly changing the subject, Dolly-Rose asks me what my mum and dad do. I talk about Mum's fudge shop and for the first time in ages I feel brave enough to talk about Dad. I don't say what he does as a job but I do say he's brilliant at daydreaming and telling stories.

"Daydreaming?" Dolly-Rose stops and looks at me. "Like Daydreaming Daisy in my book. She daydreams and tells stories."

"Yeah, I guess so," I whisper, suddenly remembering that's the book I picked up in the library – the same one Dolly-Rose has been reading, the same one she grabbed off me and didn't want me to see. "Dad was good at that. He always said it was important to dream. He used to dream that we'd live in a big house, even though we never did. And he was always telling Mum we'd have pots of cash." I laugh a bit, only it feels empty – like the biscuit jar after Topaz had been in it. "But money doesn't matter, really." I think of how I didn't tell Dad I loved him and he didn't say it back. "It's love that counts." The words get caught up behind an invisible ball in my throat.

Dolly-Rose nods her head, touches my arm and then pulls away, and it's like it never happened.

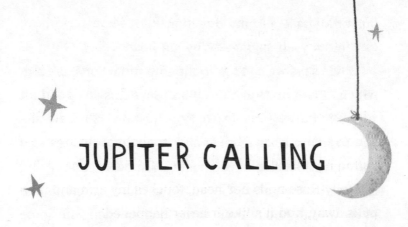

JUPITER CALLING

The programme is called *Jupiter Calling* and Gavin thinks it's out-of-this-world. He's over at our house this evening and he's put on the TV so we can watch this man talking about how incredible the universe is. Gavin's brought Maltesers. In a box. I help myself, dropping the chocolate globes into my mouth. Gavin suddenly mentions his mum taught him so many things about the universe and it's like he's said it without realizing I'm sitting beside him.

"You don't talk about her much," I reply.

"She's an incredible woman," says Gavin. "You'll have to meet her one day." He smiles and nudges the box of Maltesers in my direction.

I find myself saying, "Why not now?"

Gavin says we can't go right now and when I ask him why not, he points at the TV and says this is a good bit – the Big Bang. Terrible Topaz is upstairs. She said she had to text all her friends and it would take ages and she couldn't possibly watch any TV shows about boring things like the galaxy because she didn't care and she never would. And Mum is in the kitchen trying out some new fudge recipes for her shop, probably sea-salt flavour this time. I watch as the TV screen is dotted with speckles of stars and the voice-over tells us about how the world was created and how stars are born and die. Gavin, agreeing with everything on this programme, gives a thumbs up to the TV then tells me a joke about an astronaut's favourite chocolate being a Mars bar.

"Or a Milky Way," I say.

"Or a Galaxy."

"You'd know about that," I say, "since you're Galactic." Gavin looks confused and I burst out laughing. I can't help myself. I enjoy talking to Gavin. And I know, if Topaz was here, she'd say I shouldn't enjoy watching this programme with him as much as I am. If she comes down the stairs, she'll be so angry. As Gavin watches the TV I sneak a little look at him, wondering if this is the face of a liar. Topaz said it was. Topaz showed me the cover of her romance book, which had Summer, Autumn and the man on it, and pointed to him and said he looked just like Gavin. I said he didn't. Gavin doesn't have a full beard or a hat shaped like a pork pie or a funny tie. Topaz said he could grow one and wear the other stuff. Apparently, the man on the cover of the book had the face of a liar. I wanted to say you couldn't see his face anyway because the beard was so big, but Topaz bared her teeth and I shut up.

I glance at Gavin's eyes and he's got little crinkly laughter lines around them like crinkled chips. And his nose is a bit bumpy, like a hill you go zipping down in the snow on a bin liner and then you hit a hump right in the middle and it hurts your bum. And I can see the gold necklace glinting at his throat and as I gaze at him I wonder when he'll be marrying Blonde Ponytail Woman and if he'll have a wedding like Mum and Dad did. I wonder if Blonde Ponytail Woman will wear a crown of daisies like Mum did and if she'll dance barefoot at sunset, filled with so much happiness that she thinks she'll burst, like Mum said she did on her wedding day. For a second, I think I'd like to go to Mum and Gavin's wedding and dance barefoot, but I push the thought to the back of my mind.

"That's Cancer," says Gavin, pointing at a constellation on the TV screen.

"What do you think of getting married?" I splutter through the mushed-up Maltesers in my mouth.

Gavin stares at the TV and says, "One day." Then he grins and points at an image of Vega, which is the brightest star in the constellation of Lyra.

"One day...?"

"Yes," replies Gavin, adding, "and when I do it'll be to someone I love."

"Can you love more than one person?" My head droops and I can't believe how the words have spilled out in a surprised hurry, like sweets from a broken piñata.

"Yes." Gavin sounds certain, but then he says you can love lots of people in different ways. It's the different ways I'm worried about. What if he loves Mum a bit less than the way he loves Blonde Ponytail Woman? "Whoa! Look at that shot of space. It is epic." He shakes his head and I want to ask him straight out if he's cheating on Mum, but now the words won't come. They tangle up inside my mouth, catching on my teeth and ribboning around my tongue.

All I manage to say is, "You wouldn't lie, would you? You wouldn't lie..." I swallow. "To me?"

Gavin looks at me and his cheeks blossom red. "About what?"

I take a Malteser from the box and roll it around in my palm, telling him I don't know but it's easy to get things muddled. He tells me he's always doing that. Sometimes his words even get confused and he tells me he's not great with the chat. He rubs his nose nervously. Then he picks up a Malteser and flips it into the air and catches it in his mouth, like a seal catching a fish. After crunching it, he says he smells fudge and he wonders if there's any spare in the kitchen. Gavin eases himself off the sofa and as he disappears out the door, I think of all the questions I could have asked him. But the words have melted like the Malteser still in my palm.

"So, what's with the ugly mask?" says Topaz, suddenly appearing at the living-room door. "Oh, sorry, that's just your face." She plonks herself down on the sofa beside me. "Were you just talking to Galactic Gavin?"

I nod and then blurt out that I asked Gavin what he thought of getting married.

Terrible Topaz looks like she's sucking a giant mint with a hole in the middle.

"He said 'one day', which kind of means that—"

"It means it could be tomorrow or the next day or the

next day. It could be happening any time soon. And do you know what that means?" Topaz stares at me.

To be honest, I thought "one day" sounded like something in the distant future but Terrible Topaz says no. She tells me this is a warning and we need to see if we can bump into him and Blonde Ponytail Woman again. Urgently.

"I don't think we can go around accusing him of stuff. What if we're wrong?" I hiss, glancing at the door to make sure Gavin hasn't returned.

"We're not," launches back Topaz. "The Goblet of Truth has proved it. Let me take another look at it. We've got one more lie to go."

I tell Topaz I've left it at school because I don't want to have to explain that there's a third crack and I think it's because Mum was lying about the envelope. To be honest, I never considered the goblet could crack because of Mum. I sort of got wrapped up in Gavin because Topaz made me feel he was the only one who would tell us a lie. But he isn't.

Topaz juts out her bottom lip. "Okay, but we'll need the cup again. I suppose we could take a photo of Galactic Gavin and Blonde Ponytail Woman together. No one could argue with a photo. It would be evidence. The thing is, Mabel, we really need to sort this out once and for all because you're getting too attached to Galactic Gavin. You'll be calling him 'Dad' next."

"I will not," I say indignantly.

Mum appears in the doorway and brings in some fudge and sets it on the table in front of us. She tells us it's sea-salt flavour, as I suspected. Topaz pulls a face and asks why she'd want a mouthful of sea salt and Mum says all the best confectionary has sea salt in it these days. Mum disappears back to Gavin in the kitchen and Topaz nibbles on a corner of fudge and says it's almost as bad as that awful rose flavour Mum did before. "It was like eating petals," says Topaz, blowing a raspberry in disgust.

Fed up with everything, I tell Topaz I'm going to my room to write a poem. Only I don't write anything. Instead I lie on my bed feeling as miserable as a rainy Saturday. Downstairs I hear Gavin's mobile ring and he trots into the hallway and I hear him pull the doors closed so he can't be heard and then he comes halfway up the stairs and the phone stops ringing and I hear him grunt as he sits down. I hear him whisper, "Hey, love." I pause, straining every fibre of my being to listen. In fact, I practically superglue my ear to the wall.

"Yes, not long now. You're keeping the ring safe, aren't you? It's so special, like a piece of heaven fell to earth and ended up in this ring."

I gulp and hope Gavin can't hear my heart thundering.

"Uh-huh. I know. But I can't talk about this now because someone might hear and I don't want them to know. This is our secret. I'm thrilled that you love it. You know how special it is and what it means... I don't know what I'd do without you... I can't wait for the baby too."

Oh, Gavin.

FLUFFY

I am looking at Lee's answers on his geography test and shaking my head. Mr Spooner likes us to mark each other's work. To the question Give three ways to reduce heat loss in your house, Lee has written: Shut the windows, wear a big jumper and use the cat as a hot-water bottle. And to the question What is the strongest force on earth? Lee has written: Dóchas football team. A few minutes later, after I've put so many "x"s on Lee's paper it looks like it's covered in kisses, Mr Spooner says he will collect the work.

"Thank you everyone for trying so hard on your test," Mr Spooner says. "I'll take a look at these later.

Now, I want to move on and you're going to write poems that'll make my eyes leak."

Lee says he wouldn't want to see Mr Spooner's eyes leaking.

I glance over at Dolly-Rose. Clearly I annoyed her yesterday when we went to Mrs Latham's class, because she keeps looking at me before shaking her head and turning away. It feels like I'm on a see-saw with her – one minute it's balanced and the next I go down.

Mr Spooner continues, "I'd like you all to write about something important in your life. It can be a person, if you'd like. But it must be about something or someone big in your life. Something you can't imagine your life without. Could it be made into a final emotional poem that could float away on the breeze? Will this poem be your best yet?"

Immediately, my mind travels to Dad and his stories. Perhaps I should write a poem about worries for my final piece and let it float away. It's not exactly how Dad said it would work, but it might be worth a try. Anything is worth a try when my worries are feeling this heavy. I start off by chewing on my pencil and then I worry that I'm spending too long fretting about what to say. Then I worry I've got splinters in my mouth from chewing the pencil. Then I'm concerned about whether you can die from mouth splinters. When I look over at Dolly-Rose, she's writing in BIG BLACK CAPITAL LETTERS:

THE BLACK DOG

HE MAKES ME FEEL SAD AND HE COMES
AND GOES
BUT I DON'T LIKE HIM
I WISH HE'D GO AWAY
OR SHRINK TO THE SIZE OF A TINY BUTTON
WORN BY AN ANT
I DON'T CARE IF HE DOESN'T VISIT AGAIN
STOP VISITING MY MUM, MR BLACK DOG.
GO AWAY

BLACK DOG, BLACK DOG, GO AWAY
DON'T COME AGAIN ANOTHER DAY

I lean over and point at Dolly-Rose's poem. "Why do you want him to go away?" I whisper. "I don't understand. He looked lovely."

"I'm not telling you," says Dolly-Rose indignantly and she puts her arm over her work and tells me to mind my own business. For a second, I feel a bit wounded and then I realize Dolly-Rose doesn't have to tell me. I didn't mean to be nosy, I just wanted to be friends.

"I'm sorry," I say quickly. "You don't have to answer. I just wanted to say pets are the best." I reach over and tug on Dolly-Rose's blazer. "It would be nice if you could give your dog a chance. I guess, if you're nice to him, maybe he'll be nice in return. When I'm nice to my cat, Jupiter, he lets me stroke him, and if I'm not he scratches me or turns his back on me." I pause.

"I don't care about your cat." Dolly-Rose turns to me and her eyes are like icicles.

I say, "I know that, but I mean maybe you could see your black dog as nice and fluffy, just for a second?" I think about Gavin saying Dolly-Rose could call the dog Fluffy and how she didn't seem to like the names I gave her in the library. Maybe Fluffy is better than what I suggested. "Perhaps Gavin has a point."

It looks like Dolly-Rose still doesn't like the idea because her jaw tightens. "You were talking about the Black Dog to that Gavin person you mentioned before? The one who told you it was windy on Uranus." Dolly-Rose frowns. "It's none of his business."

"Um…" The noise vibrates on my lips. "Yes, er…

that's the same Gavin. And he likes Jupiter and he's a cat so I bet he'd like your dog, if he met it. He'd think it was fluffy and nice."

"The black dog isn't fluffy or nice and never will be and what does this Gavin know? Why would I listen to someone like him?"

"He's...he's..." I stutter. "He's fun and he talks a lot of sense. He's with my mum."

"Is he your dad?"

I shake my head and play with my fingers, like they're suddenly the most fascinating things in the entire universe. Gavin isn't my dad but for a split second I wished he was. The words were there on the tip of my tongue.

Mr Spooner's voice drifts around the classroom, telling us to finish writing our poems because he wants to take us somewhere special before the lunch break. It turns out that the "somewhere special" is not special at all and is only the playground where we'll be letting our balloons go free.

From the playground, through the railings, you can see the main road towards Dóchas High Street. To the right, the school has a big sign on the front saying *A beacon of learning* in swirly black letters. There are some hopscotch squares and a giant snake painted on the ground. Mr Spooner tries to whip up excitement by saying this balloon ceremony will be a beautiful symbol of what we've learned. Lee says it's not much of a symbol if we let our work fly away and then it gets caught on a twig in someone's garden.

"Come on," replies Mr Spooner, "where's your get-up-and-go?"

"It's got up and gone," Lee mumbles.

Mr Spooner gabbles on about how this will be amazing and how he can't wait for our parents to see what we've been up to. "I think they'll be very proud of you." My eyes stray away from Mr Spooner and out the school gates and down the road, where I see a figure with a furry hood hurrying towards town. I follow the figure until they're nothing but a polka dot in the distance. I know that person. It's Topaz. Only, I don't know why she's there instead of at school.

Topaz isn't waiting for me at the school gate today and when I get home I see she's already back, because her furry hooded coat is hanging in the hallway. I pause for a moment, staring at it, wondering if I should mention that I saw her earlier and ask why she didn't meet me this afternoon. Mum would flip if she knew Topaz wasn't in lessons. As I'm putting my coat on the hook, Mum appears in the hallway and asks if I was dawdling because Topaz made it home sooner and then points to the table and says there's a box with my name on it that Gavin dropped off earlier in the day. "It's a gift, I think. Go on, open it. I can't wait to see what it is. Do you know?" Mum's eyes glitter.

I say I don't have a clue. "He didn't say he was doing anything and it's not my birthday."

Terrible Topaz appears at the top of the stairs wearing a T-shirt that says Don't Talk to Me, I'm Not in the Mood. Clearly she is not impressed and she's mouthing that I only care about getting gifts and this isn't going to make things better.

When I open the box I see navy-blue tissue paper, and as I pull it away silver star sequins scatter everywhere. It sort of reminds me of the cover of my *I Need Space* book. Mum says she'll need to get the vacuum out. Hidden within the tissue is a small silver handheld telescope and on the side it says *SKYVIEWER 2020*. There's a note on top:

Mabel,
You mentioned you'd love to have a SKYVIEWER 2020 and I had one I got many years ago.

It was sitting in my cupboard gathering dust and when you mentioned it I went home and hunted it out. I thought you'd like it. So, here's your own telescope.

Gavin x

"Wow, it's my own SKYVIEWER 2020 – just like the one P. C. Wheeler loved."

As I run up the stairs, Topaz blocks me at the top with her hand. "Pffttt...not that stupid author again," she says, her eyebrows furrowing. That's when I notice a sparkly ring I haven't seen before. It's pretty. "I'm surprised that stupid book hasn't fallen apart. You've looked at it so many times." I feel like saying my book is a bazillion times better than her stupid romance book about Summer and Autumn, but I stop myself because Topaz's T-shirt says I shouldn't talk to her. And that's fine with me.

Later that night when I'm alone in my bedroom, I roll the SKYVIEWER 2020 around in my hand and it feels amazing. Standing in front of my window, I lift the tiny telescope up to my eye and look through the eyepiece. As I survey the stars, I feel a surge of happiness when I think of Gavin giving it to me. I've wanted this telescope for so long and now I have it and I couldn't be happier.

"You can't keep it," hisses Topaz, when she suddenly flings open my bedroom door. "We need to talk." She sighs and narrows her eyes. "It's a bribe. Maybe he knows we're onto him and this is his way of bribing you to stay quiet. It won't work." When I tell Topaz I don't agree, she leans in and jabs me with her finger and says I should.

There's the glint of a sparkle on Topaz's little finger again and my eyes follow it. "I like your ring," I say, watching it shimmer as Topaz retracts her hand. "I noticed it earlier." Topaz says it's no big deal and lots of girls have them. "Where did you get yours? Did you get it instead of coming to pick me up after school?" It's an innocent question but Topaz is like a boiling kettle, with steam spilling out and she starts marching up and down my bedroom, complaining that I'm talking about the wrong things here. It's not Topaz who's a bad person, it's Gavin, and I need to give the telescope back. Pronto!

I didn't say Topaz was a bad person. She said it herself.

My mouth's hanging open so far that I could fit a bowling ball between my lips and still have room for the world's largest boiled sweet. "But I don't want to give the telescope back," I eventually manage. "This is a special telescope. You can't buy them. I never thought I'd own one and now I do."

Topaz pauses and squints at me, then rests her hands on her hips. "Let me get this straight. Galactic Gavin comes into our lives and turns everything upside down and he's cheating on Mum and his fiancée is having a baby and has moved in with him and he's wearing her necklace and you don't care about any of it because you accept presents from him. You even..." She sighs. "*Like* him."

Topaz is right. I do. I can't help it, even though Topaz is now reminding me the goblet has proved he's lied to us. "What if the goblet is wrong or mixed up and it's cracking when other people lie and it's not perfect?" I say quietly, wishing the ground would open up and swallow me before I have to say anything else. I think about Mum lying and it makes the hairs on my arms stand to attention like tiny soldiers and I want to believe it's not possible, but part of me thinks it might be.

Topaz lets out a snort. "Is that a hypothetical question?" I have no idea what Topaz means so I nod my head. "Magic doesn't lie," she continues. "That's why it's magic. Anyway, your teacher told you the story and the goblet cracked just like he said so I'm sticking with it. And you're either with me or against me." I don't want to be against Topaz because she's so moody these days. She's been getting worse recently. I'm almost scared to talk to her in case she bites my head off. I like my head.

"I'm with you," I mumble, staring at the SKYVIEWER 2020 and wishing it could be mine for ever.

"We'll go to the estate agency and give Galactic Gavin this back," insists Topaz. "And when we've done that we don't owe him anything and it'll prove he can't bribe us with gifts. We're above bribery." Topaz thinks for a second. "Unless it was millions of gifts." She grimaces and then continues, "Here's the plan. We'll give the telescope back on Tuesday, after school. It's got to be Tuesday afternoon because that's the day he's supposed to be with his mum but we know he's with Blonde Ponytail Woman instead. We can catch him out and give him the telescope at the same time. And then we can tell Mum the whole story. Agreed?"

I nod, even though I don't want to.

THE SECRET

At the end of the school day on the following Tuesday, Topaz is waiting for me at the gates with her furry hood pulled up. She blows warmth into her hands before saying, "You've got the telescope with you, right?"

I tap my pocket and nod.

"You're totally on board with the idea that it needs to go back?"

I am about to say no when Terrible Topaz snarls at me and suddenly my mouth blurts out, "Yes."

As we wander down the road and turn into the High Street, we pass the corner shop. Topaz looks at it and then doubles back, saying she needs some chocolate before we embark on our mission. Anyone would think she was an intrepid explorer going on a year long expedition instead of nipping to the estate agency to give Gavin back a telescope.

I follow her into the shop. We're walking down the aisles when a bell tinkles behind us and I hear voices and a group of girls appear, wearing the same maroon uniform as Topaz. They look like the same girls we saw on the bus – the ones banging on the window and poking out their tongues. Topaz glances at them and looks horrified; then she ducks down, pretending she's examining the Pot Noodles.

We hear one girl say, "Mrs Flynn was so grumpy today. She gave Dylan a detention for forgetting a book. That is so strict. And Rachel just had to look at her the wrong way and she got lines. She's weird."

Someone else says, "Who? Mrs Flynn or Rachel?"

The first voice replies, "Both. But you know who is really weird in our class?" There's a pause. "Topaz."

I flick my eyes to Topaz, who gives me a goofy smile as if she doesn't know them, but the conversation continues. "I don't like her being in our class. I didn't like her from day one." I try to swallow down a knot of dismay in my throat. "She's always trying to fit in. And did you see those stupid earrings she came into school with and that glittery ring? It looked like a lump of sparkly chewing gum. And I think she made that silly friendship bracelet herself. Anyway, wait till you hear this – it's big news. I just found out a secret about her over the weekend but I can't tell a soul. My mum told me."

"What is it?" the second voice pipes up, more urgent now. "I love secrets."

"Well…" replies the girl. "I'm not sure I should tell."

I hear groaning and pleading for her to tell the story.

"But I promised my mum I wouldn't tell anyone."

More pleading follows.

"I did cross my fingers, so I suppose it cancels out the promise." There's a pause. "Okay, I'm going to tell you. But you've got to promise not to tell anyone else and you'd better show me your fingers too. No one is allowed to cross them."

There's a cough and we hear the man behind the counter asking them if they're buying or gossiping and they pick something up and then after a moment we hear the ping of the bell over the door again and they've disappeared. Topaz rises up and says she doesn't fancy a Pot Noodle today so she'll go to the chocolate section at the counter instead. After she's chosen a Twix and we've left, I turn to Topaz and ask why the girls were talking about her.

Topaz is suddenly quieter than a burger van at a vegetarian festival and she silently slips the ring off her finger and puts it in her pocket as she marches towards Yes Lets. I could swear her eyes are watering but when I ask her she mumbles, "Hay fever".

"In autumn?" I ask, chasing after her.

Through the Yes Lets window we can see Gavin sitting at his desk, talking on the phone. He's nodding away and then he laughs and picks up a brochure and looks at it and Topaz says we should go straight in and return the telescope. My fingers reach into my pocket and touch the telescope and it feels like electricity. I don't want to let it go. But there's no time like the present, according to Topaz.

I fire back, "He's not with Blonde Ponytail Woman though. I thought you wanted to catch him out first."

"Hmm...okay, that would be best," whispers Topaz. She watches as Gavin puts the phone down and turns towards the inner office door beside him. Topaz's eyes widen. We see a flash of blonde and Blonde Ponytail Woman appears. Oh, I hate it when Topaz is right. Blonde Ponytail Woman is mouthing something we can't hear and then Gavin smiles and Blonde Ponytail

Woman smiles back and then he reaches for his coat from a hook nearby.

Topaz pulls me into an alleyway beside the estate agency. "If they're putting on their coats they'll be coming out. We should stop them and give Gavin back the telescope."

"With Blonde Ponytail Woman there too?" I'm no smarty-pants but this seems like a really dopey idea to me. "But what if the shock brings on—"

"An argument?" replies Topaz. "You're right. He'll have to tell her we're Mum's kids and then there will be a big argument in the street. Or what if he's onto us and he's planned out what lies to tell us and he says she's his sister or something?"

"I was thinking more like the shock could bring on the baby."

Topaz grabs me by the arm and sucks air in through her teeth, saying she hadn't thought of that and she'd be no good at delivering a baby in the street when she can't even deliver her maths homework on time. Meanwhile, the door of the agency swings open and closes again and by the time we've peeped out from the alleyway, Gavin and Blonde Ponytail Woman are walking towards the jewellery shop.

Blonde Ponytail Woman goes into Throwing Rocks

and comes out a few seconds later with a little bag in her hand. She speaks to Gavin, opens the bag and pulls out something that glints. Then she beckons to Gavin to help her put on a necklace. Beside me, Topaz is muttering that she knew it – she knew Blonde Ponytail Woman would have a matching gold necklace. "I bet it's got his name on it. Autumn had one of those in my book."

"A necklace with his name on it?"

Topaz shakes her head like a dog with a flea in its ear, "Not with Galactic Gavin's name, but *her* boyfriend's name."

I don't mind admitting, my insides have turned to sludge and another worry goes straight into the worry suitcase. It hurts me to say it but it looks like Topaz is right again.

Meanwhile, Topaz is wittering on about how Blonde Ponytail Woman must have put the necklace into the jeweller's to get it engraved and now she's wearing it, and I start to think how maybe Galactic Gavin really isn't one hundred per cent nice like I thought. What if he's not even ninety-nine per cent nice? Or fifty per cent? What if it's below fifty? It's almost too horrible to think about, but Topaz seems so convinced that she's making me question myself.

A bit further down the road, Gavin and Blonde Ponytail Woman suddenly stop outside a grocery shop. I hold my breath before whispering, "What if they're doing a weekly shop now?" Then I remind Topaz that it takes Mum an hour to do one of those. Topaz tells me to shut up and watch and as we do Gavin ducks into the grocery shop and comes out a couple of minutes later with a bunch of white flowers. He hands them to Blonde Ponytail Woman.

I look at Topaz and she looks at me.

Then we glare at Gavin.

Eventually Topaz manages to hiss, "OMG. He's bought her flowers. They're probably...um...expensive roses or something and he doesn't buy Mum flowers at all." Gavin does buy Mum flowers, but Topaz has conveniently forgotten. "That's it, I can't look." She does look though, through her outspread fingers, and then she drags me down the road after them, ducking in and out of shop doors in case they turn around.

Five minutes later, Blonde Ponytail Woman and Gavin take a right turn and we do too. I tell Topaz we can't follow them too far or we'll be late home and Mum will worry and then she'll be annoyed and start texting me in capital letters. Topaz says we're okay for ten or fifteen minutes and we should keep observing what's going on for a while like they do on police dramas.

Gavin and Blonde Ponytail Woman stop at a large grey building on Buckingham Place and I remember that this is the street where Dolly-Rose lives. The house Gavin stops in front of is called The Fir Trees and he ushers Blonde Ponytail Woman inside, letting her go first.

"Can we go now?"

"No, we're observing," says Topaz, although I'm not entirely sure what we can find out from staring at the outside of a house.

They've not been inside five minutes when they both come out again and we hear them calling that they forgot to get some sweets when they were in the shop.

"Where did the flowers go? Who are they calling to?" hisses Topaz, pulling me down behind a hedge. When I tell her I don't have a clue, she says she's going to find out. After Gavin and Blonde Ponytail Woman have walked off down the road, Topaz jumps up and runs up to the front door of The Fir Trees. Before I can stop her, she's ringing the doorbell and it parps. A woman appears behind the glass and, staring at us, she opens the door.

"Who are you?" asks Topaz, confused.

The woman laughs and says that she works here and

keeps things running smoothly, not that it's any of our business. In fact, she does just about everything.

Next Topaz asks, "Is this Carina's house? Are you running it for her?" She whispers in my ear that Carina is definitely Blonde Ponytail Woman's name.

The woman thinks for a second and then says, "Carina, Carina. Ah, Carina. I get you now. I wasn't sure who you were talking about. Yes, she lives here along with the others." She smiles at us and Topaz winks at me to confirm she was right. Then she jolts when she realizes what the woman has said.

"Lives here? The others?" Topaz's eyes have narrowed. "There are other women here with Carina?"

The woman replies, "Oh, yes, quite a few."

"And they all know Gavin?" Topaz's mouth drops open and if Nana Anna was here she'd say she could catch more than a few flies in there.

"Do you mean Gavin Bickerstaff?" the woman asks. Topaz nods. "Yes, he's lovely. They all adore him here. But it's Carina he comes to see." The woman winks at Topaz and then tells us she has things to do so she needs to get back. Slowly she closes the door on The Fir Trees and Topaz stands there with her mouth still hanging open like she's catching flies.

"This is a love *dodecahedron*," Topaz eventually

manages as we walk back down Buckingham Place. "It's not a triangle at all. It's so much worse than I thought. Galactic Gavin has *loads* of girlfriends."

"I don't think he can have loads of girlfriends because the lady at the door said he was only interested in Carina, didn't she? She's the one he wants to see." I shrug.

As we turn right and wander towards home, Topaz clutches my arm and tells me one woman is bad enough and this is more proof than she ever expected. Then she tuts and says she forgot to get a photo. "And you still can't keep that telescope," she mutters.

"You're supposed to keep gifts and cherish them, otherwise it's rude," I say to Topaz. But she tells me that I don't keep Jupiter's gifts.

"They're dead!" I squeal.

Topaz takes off down the road and I'm dragging behind her, past the tiny houses on Bartlett Road and then turning into Carnation Street where the Bluebell Estate starts. As I'm crossing the road I realize there is someone sitting in a garden area and she's reading a book that looks familiar and I think she looks sad. I watch as she turns a page, sighs and then closes her eyes as though she's daydreaming.

"Daydreaming Daisy," I mumble.

A voice drifts from an open window, shouting, "Dinner's nearly ready."

That's when the girl shouts, "Okay, Mum," and sets down the book. And that's when I notice her twiddling her copper plaits. Here's the odd thing, it's Dolly-Rose and I wonder why she is in the wrong place, in front of the wrong house, in the wrong street.

Later that night, I can't get to sleep and I reach for my star book like I've done so many times before. As I flick through the pages I hear footsteps and there's a tiny knock at my door. It opens slightly and Terrible Topaz says she can't sleep either. I budge up in the bed and she jumps in beside me.

In the half-light I see something glitter on her wrist. "What's that?"

"A bracelet."

"Is it new?"

"Maybe," mumbles Topaz. Then she whispers, "Reading that book again." She pulls my duvet up to her chin. "This P. C. Wheeler must be an amazing astronomer if you keep reading it over and over. You wouldn't catch me ever asking about the stars. They're boring. Who cares?"

"I do," I say. "It's important to me. The book's important."

"Do you know what's really important?" whispers Topaz. "Telling Mum about Galactic Gavin. Making sure her heart isn't broken. I think we've got to do it. We must tell Mum tomorrow."

"Tomorrow…"

"Tomorrow." Terrible Topaz lets out a grunt and then I pause, listening to her breathe.

"Do you wish Dad was here?" The words spill out like Smarties from an upturned tube. Right this minute, I feel like the worry suitcase is about to burst open. Swallowing deeply, I think I might be able to share one of my worries with Topaz. "Things might be different. Like, he could tell us a story right now," I whisper. "Remember how he said our worries would float away like dandelion clock seeds?" I sigh, hugging the dark, my breathing coming in short ragged bursts. "Topaz, I've wanted to tell you this for a while. I'm worried about Mum. I think something is going on." I can hardly believe I've told Topaz this but recently the worry suitcase has been so heavy that I've felt I'm going to drop under the weight. Having shared my worry, I wait for Topaz to answer but she doesn't. I pause, breathing in and out – wondering if I should say this. A second

211

later I whisper, "I saw an envelope, Topaz." I pause again. "I thought it was written by Dad. But Mum said it wasn't anything important and that's when the Goblet of Truth cracked for the third time and I didn't tell you." My mouth feels like I've eaten a load of dry crackers and I try to swallow. "What if Mum is lying? What if it's not just Gavin keeping things from us? I've been worrying about that."

Topaz shifts position and I can feel her freezing feet on mine and I pull away. My eyes are fixed on the walls dotted with tiny stars from my constellation light and I swallow and take a huge breath. This is it! This is the moment I'm going to tell Topaz – it feels right. I think back to number four on my list of worries and then the words tumble out. "I worry that I have a worry suitcase, Topaz. And I can't speak to anyone about it because no one would understand." I pause before filling the silence, "And it's not like a proper suitcase you can see, because it's inside my head. Sometimes the worries make my tummy hurt and my throat feel like it's got a lump in there that won't go. But I'm speaking to you about it now, Topaz. Do you have a worry suitcase too? Please tell me you understand?"

Topaz lets out a little snore.

"The Worry Suitcase"

by Mabel Mynt

I have a suitcase right now
Here with me at home
I don't want it somehow
It won't leave me alone
It's with me in class
It's there when I wake
The suitcase won't go
There's no route I can take

There's no eye that can see
That suitcase of mine
I wish I was free
I wish it was fine
I know what's inside
The worries are there
It's heavy to carry
It feels so unfair

The suitcase is clever
I know it won't go
It's staying for ever
And maybe that's so
That the suitcase is mine
And we never can part
Yet the weight of the suitcase
Is breaking my heart

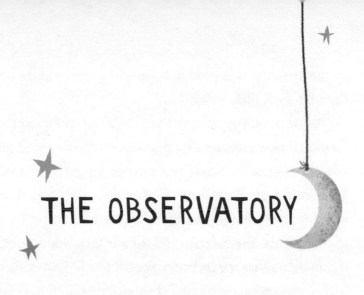

THE OBSERVATORY

The next day, just before lunch, and while I'm worrying about what Topaz is going to say to Gavin and Mum later, Mr Spooner's face drops and he says he wants to talk to us about something important. It's about not borrowing books from his shelf without writing our names in the borrowing book. "It's not the worst thing in the world, but I'd prefer it if you'd give me the heads up if you want to take a book. So, while I'm discussing this, I'd like to mention that I'm missing my copy of *Myths, Mystery, Magic* and I would very much like to have it back. That way, you can all enjoy reading it, but you have to return it if you do borrow it."

Startled, I look up and Mr Spooner glances at me and then his eyes flick away.

"Anyway, if you've got the book, my door will be open at lunchtime and I'd appreciate it if you could just pop it back on the shelf. It's easy to forget that it's in your locker or at the bottom of your school bag. Then in future, please put your name in the borrowing book. If you put the book back, you'll be in my Good Books. If you don't, you might find yourself in my Bad Books."

I hope Mr Spooner doesn't think I've taken it. I read the section about the goblet and then made sure the book went straight back on his bookshelf and I didn't borrow it again.

But someone has.

When the bell goes, everyone dodges round the desks and runs to the door like tigers chasing zebras. Mum has packed me a Penguin biscuit and I'm pulling off the wrapper in the playground when I spy Dolly-Rose acting a bit suspiciously. It's not like she's tiptoeing around or anything, but she's in the corner of the playground, rummaging around in her bag, and she looks furtively to her left and right to make sure no one is watching before she pulls out a book. I can't read the title from where I'm sitting but I recognize it. It's *Myths, Mystery, Magic*. The missing book from Mr Spooner's shelf. Dolly-Rose flicks the book under her blazer and moves swiftly across the playground towards our classroom. One more glance behind her and she opens the classroom door and sneaks inside and then reappears seconds later and runs off as though nothing has happened.

The Penguin is half in my mouth, half hanging out. I take a bite and then chew, but my mind is a merry-go-round. Why did Dolly-Rose take the book and why was she so interested in reading about my goblet when she told me to my face that she wasn't bothered about it at all?

That afternoon, Galactic Gavin turns up at our house at 4.15 precisely and says he is taking us all out as a treat. "It's something out of this world."

Topaz rolls her eyes and hisses at me that it doesn't matter where we go, we still need to tell Mum the truth about him. "Huh? Out of this world? I'm glad I'm not going to have to put up with him any longer. We need to tell Mum about his cheating tonight, whatever happens. Yes?"

I don't reply, which Topaz takes as a yes anyway.

Gavin stands in the living room, grinning. He's

wearing a heavy dark coat and has a bag slung over his shoulder. He tells us to get ourselves ready, because he has a surprise for us. Mum claps her hands together and says she loves surprises.

"It's nothing to the surprise we've got for Galactic Gavin," Topaz mutters, scowling and nudging me.

I ignore her and dash upstairs, flinging my blazer on the floor. I notice the goblet falls out of my pocket, but I don't have time to pick it up because Mum is shouting at me to hurry up. Instead I leave it there and dump my school books beside it, before changing out of my school uniform and dropping that on the floor too.

We're out the door within ten minutes and as we bundle into Gavin's car Topaz asks where we're going.

"Ah," replies Gavin, turning the steering wheel. "I told you it was out of this world. Start guessing."

Topaz squirms a bit in the back seat and I hear her grunt.

Gavin and Mum are chatting all the way down the road in the car. We pass the High Street and The Fir Trees and Gavin lets out a tiny cough, which Topaz totally notices and she says to me it's a sign. But Mum seems so happy that I don't feel comfortable doing this to her, even though Terrible Topaz has the whole situation all whipped up and she's convinced that Gavin is the worst person on earth or any other planet.

After Gavin's parked the car and we get out, I look up at the darkening sky. I can see my breath mingle in tiny cotton-wool balls with the late afternoon air. "Isn't this amazing?" says Mum, turning back to grin at us. "Isn't Gavin lovely?" Topaz grunts again and Mum rolls her eyes and I hear her mumble something like "Kids, eh?" to Gavin and then something about them being "another species."

The four of us hurry away from the car through the town park and then stop as Gavin declares, "We're here." He points to Dóchas Observatory in the distance. "It's out of this world – like I promised. I love it. It's a place where you can always find me." He smiles and winks.

"Always?" I grin back. Gavin nods and I stare, wide-eyed with wonder, at the observatory in front of me, because I've always wanted to go there. I'm so happy I could hug him, but I don't because Topaz would be so angry.

"Wow," I whisper, my eyes scanning the dome, which looks like half a wheel of cheese.

Topaz leans in and says, "Don't forget what we have to do later. We must tell Mum about him. It can't go on any longer. You're getting attached to a cheat, Mabel."

"I'm not," I say indignantly, but my eyes never leave the dome.

"You are," Topaz hisses. "I'm putting an end to all this tonight. I've told you."

I've already stopped listening to Topaz, because we're rushing through the park again and then up the steps and my chest is swelling with happiness. For once, I've forgotten the invisible suitcase I'm carrying as we reach the front door.

The inside of the building is beautiful and there are mosaic tiles on the floor and they're dark blue and every so often there's a golden six-pointed star and I find myself playing hopscotch on them. When Mum calls me over we go to the ticket office and Gavin gives the man his name and says there were tickets left for him. The man ducks down behind the counter and then passes Gavin an envelope, saying, "The tickets are inside. I hope you and your family enjoy it, sir." Gavin gives a little dip of the head but doesn't respond and as we wander away he looks at Topaz and me and says he hopes it didn't annoy us that the man thought we were his family.

"It *did* annoy me," mumbles Topaz. "We're not family. We already have a dad."

"Topaz," snaps Mum. Gavin says it's all right and

220

he's sorry again about the mistake the man made. I don't say anything because it felt sort of nice that the man thought we were a family and my tummy didn't feel in a knot, for once – it felt okay. Gavin says he knows he's not our dad and he'd never dream of trying to replace someone so precious to us. Topaz is still grumbling in the background but I find myself whispering to Gavin that it's no problem, mistakes happen. He gives me a grateful smile and hooks his arm into mine.

From the corner of my eye, I can see Topaz seething again. Her face is all blotchy and she's signalling that I should unhook myself and I do, but I don't feel so good as I did a minute ago.

The observatory is split into different areas, but we go straight to the planetarium, which is the first turning on the left. Gavin says we won't have time to take everything in before the place shuts, but we can come another day to see the exhibits in the other rooms. The man at the door checks our tickets and tells us to go inside. He says there is a special guest introducing a film about the galaxy.

"They show the film on the dome," he says, pointing upwards. "And the seats are very comfortable too."

"Fabulous," says Mum, only I can't tell if it's because

she's excited about the film or the comfortable seats. As we enter the large domed room, Mum is hanging onto Gavin and her eyes are all twinkly and happy and she's grinning so much that it makes me smile too. But Topaz isn't happy and I don't even need to look at her to know that, because I can feel her waves of annoyance crashing over me.

When we find a seat and after the audience has settled, a woman walks onstage and introduces herself as Patience Gambo, Dóchas Observatory's own astronomer. As she stands in front of the microphone, I feel a shiver of anticipation gallop across my arms. I want to be Patience Gambo. I want to stand in front of an audience saying the words she's saying. When I grow up I'll be an astronomer, just like her and P. C. Wheeler.

At first Patience talks about her background and just as she's getting to an interesting bit, Gavin nips off to the toilet, telling us he's got a bladder like a sieve. Which is too much information, according to Topaz, who says she has a bladder like a camel. Which might be right because Mum often says that Topaz has got the hump. I barely watch him go because my eyes are fixed on Patience and my ears are tuned into her too, listening to how she was inspired to be an astronomer by a book that her father gave her. I hold my breath and then she says, "It was *I Need Space* by P. C. Wheeler."

"That's my book!" I say, grabbing Mum by the arm. Mum smiles.

"It's no longer in print," says Patience Gambo and then she goes on to tell us that there's a very special guest in the audience, but she won't name the person because they'd be too embarrassed. I look around, wondering who it is, and although the room is full no one moves. Clearly, the very special person doesn't want to be spotted. Topaz leans over and asks if I think it's a celebrity – the Queen or a princess or maybe a singer. I tell her I don't have a clue but I'm not sure the Queen would be in Dóchas Observatory.

"Maybe it's me," says Topaz. "I'm a VIP."

Very Irritating Person, I think to myself.

Gavin reappears and sits down in his seat just as Patience Gambo says, "Together we will travel on a journey of billions of years. We will see new life – the birth of a star – and we will witness its death. We will feel hope like we have never felt before. Space is behind us and space is before us – let us watch the heavens unfold and let us discover how the stars are in our souls. Let us feel their magnificence in every fibre of our being. You are a child of the cosmos…"

There's a round of applause from everyone (except Topaz, who is playing with her new glittery bracelet) as everything goes dark and then the dome comes alive, scattered with a multitude of stars, and the music swells and I let the stars sink into my soul for the next hour. We see all the stars and constellations from Antares to Zibal, and when it finishes I feel like I'm floating on a carpet of space dust as I leave the room.

Gavin looks over at me and asks if I enjoyed it and I say it was cosmic and it really was. Gavin agrees and says he loves it so much he's always here. He laughs again – clearly it's a private joke, but I just don't get it. And then he says that this place is special.

For a moment, I feel a wave of happiness. But it soon disappears when Topaz whispers, "The time is coming. Tick-tock. Tick-tock..."

THE METEORITE

As we wander away from the observatory, Gavin says we should jump in the car and head back to Dóchas, but it might be nice to do a little detour to the lough and point out all the stars we learned about in the observatory now that it's properly dark. "Should we?" Gavin looks at Mum.

She grins. "Okay, let's."

Gavin takes off like he's taking part in the Grand Prix. When we get near the lough, he pulls up and parks and then goes into the boot and takes out a blanket and grabs his bag. We climb up the steep hill that overlooks the lough and when we reach the top, near Dóchas

225

Rock, I think of Dad and his bedtime stories. I ache for a little fist bump and for Dad to tell me that he loves me, but instead Gavin is telling me to lay the blanket down. He throws it to me and I catch it and he smiles and tells me to give him a high five, which I do. It's not quite a fist bump but it makes me laugh anyway. Next, Gavin tells us we should have some hot chocolate. He brings a flask out of his bag and four cups and asks who wants one.

"Me," I say enthusiastically.

Topaz grunts.

Gavin pours a stream of milky hot liquid into the cups and passes them around and I take a sip and feel instantly warm inside, like a kitten has curled up on top of me and is keeping me toasty. Topaz sips her hot chocolate reluctantly and Gavin asks her if the drink is okay and she mumbles that it's going to take more than hot chocolate to win her over.

I set my cup down and lie back and look up into the sky. And Gavin tells me stories all about Saturn and Mercury and how much he loves talking about the universe. "I miss it," he whispers. But I'm not sure what he means when he can talk about it anytime he likes.

Far below us, the town twinkles with lights and the lough beyond is a dark, shimmering sheet. Occasionally it glitters under the stars and high above us a shooting star zips across the sky. "It's like a free fireworks display," says Mum, nuzzling into Gavin's chest. A second later, he reaches into his bag and says he's got another gift for me, promising that he has a present for Topaz too, but he couldn't carry it with him.

"You wouldn't want this one anyway, Topaz," laughs Gavin. He tells me to open my hand and I do and he places a small stone in my palm.

Topaz sneers it's nothing more than a bit of shabby rock.

"It's a meteorite," corrects Gavin. "I found it a long time ago not far from here and my mum told me all about it and that's what got me interested in space. At first you think it's just a stone, but then you discover it's incredible. It's like a piece of heaven fell to earth." *Like a piece of heaven fell to earth and ended up in this ring?* I swallow, remembering what Gavin said when he was on the phone. "This is only a third of it. One piece is somewhere else and I've got the final part."

"It's beautiful."

"It is not," huffs Topaz.

But it is. It's a beautiful piece of space rock and it's here in my palm. Gavin grins and says he thinks it's amazing too. "I guess it was up there with Saturn and the planets once upon a time and now it's here with us. It took a long journey to get to where it belongs now. But it's loved and just as incredible as it was before. It's just in a different place."

Topaz says, "That meteorite started off looking lovely and shiny and now it's nothing but a lump of cold, hard stone. You see, we don't like things that start off glittery but turn out to be a pile of p—"

"Pluto!" I shout, pointing into the sky.

Topaz gives me the side-eye and then continues, "And you know what's worse? When you believe in that lovely thing and then it turns out that it's horrible and it's only pretending to shine. So, you decide that it's best to get rid of it."

My stomach falls to the bottom of the steep hill as Gavin stares at Topaz, confused. Mum is trying to smile but I think she's perplexed too. She gives a nervous laugh. I'm worried about what's going to happen next, so I keep trying to talk about Uranus and black holes.

"Please," I hiss to Topaz when I've finished rabbiting on. "Not now." Not when I've forgotten the worry suitcase for hours. I don't want to spoil the moment, because I've enjoyed the whole evening so much, it seems a shame to destroy it when we could do this another day. Maybe we should say what we have to say on a rainy day when it's already horrible and it's like the sky is crying.

But nothing is going to stop Topaz being terrible.

"Mum, I hate to tell you this, but have you seen Galactic, I mean, Gavin's necklace?"

Mum looks as Gavin stretches his neck to show her and then he runs his fingers through his hair, saying that the necklace isn't a secret.

"That's odd," says Topaz, arching her eyebrow. "Because it has a woman's name on it, doesn't it? It isn't just a constellation – isn't that the truth? There's more to it than that. You know someone called Carina."

Uh-oh. Topaz has totally put Jupiter among the pigeons now.

Gavin's cheeks simmer and then boil. "Um...yes, it's both. It's a woman's name *and* it's a constellation "

Topaz is in full flight now and saying that's not all – there's more. "You've been spotted with another woman, someone who isn't Mum."

Mum looks at Gavin, quizzically. "Another woman?"

"And Mum, it's not just one woman, there are others too. I was *told* that there were others. Isn't that right, Mabel?"

"Don't bring me into it," I mumble. Topaz is in full "terrible" mode now and she's nudging me, wild-eyed, and telling Mum that she can't divulge her sources but they're reputable.

"I didn't want to bring this up, Mum," says Topaz and there's a pained expression on her face. "But I have to."

Gavin is looking at us and saying, "I don't have a clue who all these sources are or what women you're talking about and I promise I'm not dating anyone else. You've got me all wrong. I wouldn't date anyone else – I think you're confused." He looks at Topaz but she's shaking her head, the pained expression giving way to something a bit smug.

Mum flushes and takes a sip from her cup. "I'm not sure my girls would be confused." She raises an eyebrow and makes a little "humphf" sound at the same time. I know it's a danger sign because she did the same to me when I had to own up and say I got chocolate on her new rug and it wasn't actually Jupiter's upset belly like I'd pretended.

Gavin bubbles on about how we're not confused then but mistaken and he's not criticizing us but there's been a mix-up and he doesn't know why. "I can't explain it," he adds, throwing his hands up in the air. "I do see people every day but I don't love them. I mean, in my job I meet women all the time, but I don't love them and they don't love me," he echoes.

"You say that," says Topaz. "But we've seen you with a woman. We've seen you buy her flowers."

"Flowers?" Mum's eyebrow goes higher.

"And presents," continues Topaz.

"Presents?" Mum's eyebrow is so high now that you can hardly see it.

"I don't buy women presents," says Gavin. "Or flowers. Unless it's my mum."

"It wasn't your mum," adds Topaz. "And you buy jewellery."

"Jewellery?" Mum's eyebrow has disappeared into her hair now.

"A ring," declares Topaz.

"A ring?" repeats Mum.

"Did you or did you not buy a ring recently, Gavin?" Topaz looks at him.

There's a pause. "Yes," says Gavin, fidgeting.

"So, the woman is your fiancée," mutters Topaz. "And you live with her and she's having your baby and..."

Gavin interrupts, "No, I don't have a fiancée who's having my baby." A vein pulses at the side of his forehead and I can hear him breathing through his nose. As I stare at him a rocket of red whooshes up his cheeks and he gives a hard smile. "My sister is pregnant, but that's it. There's no fiancée." Gavin shakes his head indignantly before saying this is ridiculous and he won't be part of it.

Topaz snorts.

"Why would my girls make this up?" Mum is giving Gavin the hard stare and any second now I think she's about to blow. "Are they making up the story about a ring?"

Gavin says he *has* bought a ring. His shoulders droop and he clasps his hands so tightly together that his knuckles whiten.

"So, they're telling the truth about that?"

Gavin nods. Mum waits for an explanation but Gavin doesn't have one. All he says is he's not getting married or having a baby and he could explain about the ring but this isn't the right time.

"Not the right time to tell me you've been buying another woman a ring?"

Gavin looks at Mum. "It's not the right time to explain because I can see you're angry with me. But I am telling the truth." Gavin looks at me and then Topaz and he repeats, "I'm telling the truth and I want you to believe me. I did buy a ring. But this isn't about that. It's about you believing me and knowing I wouldn't lie to you about stuff as important as this."

Mum suddenly looks wounded and instead of being furious she rises and tells us it's time we left. She turns to Gavin and her voice tight as the lid on a jar, hisses, "I've been deceived before and it hurt and I promised myself I'd never let it happen again. Not with anyone." Gavin opens his mouth to say something and Mum echoes, "I'm never letting it happen again, do you understand?"

With that, she marches us down the hill with cups of cold chocolate in our hands. Gavin shouts for us to wait but we don't. Mum keeps on walking with her head held high and she tells us to do the same and not look back. I feel the meteorite, sharp in my hand, and I think how all the fun we were having earlier has evaporated. And the worry suitcase is back and we need to walk home because we came in Gavin's car and I know I'm going to have to drag that suitcase of worries all the way there.

When we reach the front door, Mum asks Topaz what she saw and Topaz replies, "I'm sorry, Mum. I saw Gavin proposing to a woman with a ring. She put it on her finger."

Mum smiles. "Thank you, Topaz. That's all I needed to hear."

Later when we're in Topaz's bedroom, Topaz says, "We couldn't put up with it any longer. You heard Mum. She promised herself not to let anyone deceive her again. We made sure that Gavin didn't do that."

"Okay," I say slowly. "But it wasn't nice. It made me feel sad. I think Mum might have loved him."

"She didn't," replies Topaz. "But maybe you did, a bit, by the end."

I don't answer because I *did* like him. He was fun to be around, he liked stars and he joined in with everything and he was good at making constellation lights. And when he was around I felt safe and I'd even started having fun again. He *was* one hundred per cent nice. Was...

When I get to my bedroom I switch on Gavin's constellation light and it throws stars across the wall and I feel a wave of sadness. And my heart is so sore it feels like it needs a sticking plaster fit for a T-rex to make it better. Worry after worry rains down on me, making my breath come in short gasps. From my bed I can hear Mum in her bedroom and she's blowing her nose and sniffing. She sniffs again and I know she's probably upset and there's nothing I can do and Gavin's words swirl around in my head like a never-ending Mr Whippy ice cream. He kept saying he was telling the truth.

That's when I remember that I left the Goblet of Truth on my floor somewhere. I'm about to look for it when I spy Jupiter with something glinting under his paw, and he's guarding whatever it is like one of his victims. I stoop down and see it's the Goblet of Truth. Quickly I reach for it, avoiding Jupiter's claws, and I double-check if there have been any changes. There have! The first crack has healed. Which means there was a truth and even if the goblet wasn't with me when I heard it, it looks like the magic has still worked.

Gavin was telling us the truth, the goblet proves it. I feel a surge of relief. And then I'm determined to clear Gavin's name.

THE MISSING GOBLET

Gavin doesn't come back to our house on Thursday or Friday or over the weekend. It feels like when Dad left, like there's a foggy cloud hanging over everything. I was sure Gavin would return the next day – just like I imagined Dad would. But he didn't. Then I thought he'd come back the day after. But Gavin hasn't returned.

Mum's been terribly miserable. Last night she accidentally set an extra place at the table for him and then remembered and cleared it away again. The chair sat empty and all I could do was sit looking at it while I ate my potato waffles. We didn't talk about stars. We didn't talk much at all. Mum's stopped trying new fudge recipes too. No more special flavours simmering away in a saucepan, no more using Gavin as a fudge-tasting guinea pig with a huge appetite. Mum is back to sitting in her dressing gown, staring into space.

This morning, Mum forgot to give me my lunch and I had to go back and get it. I found her sniffing and wiping her nose and when I asked if she was okay she said she was. I shook my head and pointed to her streaming nose and she pretend-sneezed, a big *A-wish-oo*, and said she had a cold. But I wasn't convinced.

Before the morning bell, I'm sitting on the school wall, worrying about how bad things have become. Dad's gone, Gavin's gone, Mum lied about a letter from Dad and Topaz's mood is worse than ever and she can't blame that on Gavin. Dolly-Rose slides up beside me and sits down, saying, "My dad is a nuclear scientist. Do you know what that means?"

I shrug.

"It means he's very clever and he studies stuff. Um... nuclear stuff."

I blink. "Oh, right."

"He won a prize once," says Dolly-Rose, smoothing down her pleated skirt.

"For his nuclear work?"

"No, in school for a drawing of an alien." Dolly-Rose smiles.

I find myself smiling too. "I thought you were annoyed and not speaking to me."

Dolly-Rose shakes her head. "Annoyed? I'm not annoyed. You looked annoyed before I came over but I made you smile. You made me smile once."

"I did?"

"When you spoke about Gavin. Remember, you said he told you lots of interesting things, like it's windy on Uranus. I think Gavin sounds like fun."

"Oh yes, he is." I pause, thinking for a second, before adding, "Mum isn't feeling herself at the minute." I don't say it's because of Gavin.

Dolly-Rose whispers, "My mum's like that sometimes too." We sit in silence for a while, watching the wind play catch with a crisp packet. Dolly-Rose leans down and tugs at her sock before straightening back up. Her eyes close for a second and then she twirls the end of her plait before letting it drop.

"But your mum's a brain surgeon," I eventually manage. "So, I bet she has a lot on her mind."

"She does have a lot on her mind," offers Dolly-Rose. "But she's not really a brain surgeon..."

I knew it! This is it! Dolly-Rose is going to admit what I found out – that her mother tiles bathrooms for a living and that it's okay.

"Does she work with tiles?" I whisper, urging her into answering.

"Tiles? No, she's a..." Dolly-Rose stutters and looks panicked and I feel awful because it's obvious she's uncomfortable. "She's a..." She takes a breath and it looks painful. "She's a..."

"A mum?" I say and Dolly-Rose gives me a half smile, relieved she doesn't have to say anything else.

She plays with her fingers for a moment before adding, "I try to help when Mum's not feeling okay, you know."

I stare at Dolly-Rose, my eyes wide. Obviously, she's trying to say something important to me, but I don't know exactly what. I tell her that it's good to help, only Dolly-Rose shrugs and says she doesn't think it makes much difference sometimes.

The silence returns so I pick at a soggy leaf on my shoes. When I flick it away I offer, "I'm sure it does."

"What would you know?" Dolly-Rose suddenly changes again. Horrible Dolly-Rose has returned and instantly it feels like I'm treading on eggshells with her and I'm probably going to break enough to make a giant omelette.

"I know plenty," I fire back, angry that her mood has changed so quickly. "I know that you were the person who borrowed *Myths, Mystery, Magic* last week. What did you want it for?"

Dolly-Rose sighs and then gets up and says she doesn't have a clue about that book or anything about the chapter on Rún. Then she says she's got her own book to read and I don't know what she's going through. I look at her and say that she's always telling me her life is perfect, so what has she got to complain about? Dolly-Rose says that's what people always say and they're all wrong. "It doesn't matter what you do or where you live," she spits. "It doesn't matter how much you daydream or how perfect your life seems to everyone else on the outside, because the black dog can still turn up."

"I don't feel like talking about your dog," I say fiercely. "Go back to reading your *Daydreaming Daisy* book, seeing as that's all you ever seem to do, and leave me alone."

Dolly-Rose glares at me and says I know nothing about daydreaming and what it means to her, then walks away.

I didn't say I did.

Later that morning, Mr Spooner says we're going to write our final poem today and then he'll collect in all the cards and read them and judge which is the best and deserving of being a winner. He also tells us he's going to go pick up the helium balloons next week and then it all gets very exciting because we can pick a balloon and attach our finished poems to it. So, I'm supposed to be writing my poem, but instead I've pulled the golden goblet from my pocket and I'm studying it and the remaining two cracks, tilting it this way and that. *Two more truths to come*, I tell myself, watching as the light catches on the surface.

"Mabel, are you staring at the Goblet of Truth? We've already discussed that myth, which means you shouldn't have it on your table now. That chat is over. Bring it to me, please."

There is no point arguing with a teacher, because you cannot win. I take the cup to Mr Spooner and he sets it on his shelf. He tells me I can get it at lunchtime and after that he doesn't want to see it again.

The cup sits there all the way through history. It sits there while Mr Spooner tells us he couldn't find anyone to do the countdown for the balloon release after all. No celebrities or pillars of the community.

There's a groan.

"At first..." adds Mr Spooner. "I couldn't find a person *at first*. But then..."

There's a whoop.

"I found someone who would be passionate about this. The idea came to me last night."

There's a double-whoop.

"This person is known to you all."

There's a whoop-whoop-whoop and Lee is saying the person must be really famous if we all know them.

"And he's given up his time and you won't believe it... it's me." Mr Spooner claps his hands together.

The cup sits there through the lesson on writing our poems. It sits there when Mr Spooner talks about positivity changing the world. Since I wasn't very positive to Dolly-Rose, I lean over and tell her I'm sorry if she thinks I was being irritating. "I didn't mean to upset you. I only told you to go back to reading your book and daydreaming. It's not a big deal."

"I know," says Dolly-Rose. "But you don't understand."

"I might."

Dolly-Rose's eyes drop and she plays with her fingers. She tells me that it's nice to escape and that sometimes that's what she does when she's reading a book. "I can be anyone or go anywhere. I don't have to worry when I'm reading." Without warning, her eyes turn to steel. "Anyway, like I said, you wouldn't understand, but I'm going to sort it all out. I know what I need to do."

The thing is, I might not understand some of what she's saying, but I understand about worrying all right.

I'm about to say so when the fire alarm goes off. Mr Spooner says it's just a drill and can we all line up, so we do. I'm at the front of the queue and Dolly-Rose hangs back. Mr Spooner directs us out of the classroom into the playground and tells us where to stand.

Dolly-Rose saunters out of the classroom like she's got all the time in the world and Mr Spooner tells her to hurry up because she wouldn't have time to mess around if it was a real fire. We wait in the playground with all the other classes and we're chattering like we're chimps at a tea party. Dolly-Rose doesn't join in; instead, she leans against the big tree in the playground.

The fire drill takes so long that it slips into lunchtime and Mr Spooner excuses us, saying now it's over we can go get our lunch boxes or school dinners. Nobody speaks to me at lunch and I've lost the straw for my orange juice carton and that's another thing that bugs me.

The day doesn't get any better. After lunch when Mr Spooner has taken in all our poetry cards I ask him for my goblet back, because I didn't get a chance at lunchtime thanks to the fire drill. He looks around for it and says it must have been misplaced because it's not where he left it, but he's sure it'll be around because magic cups don't just disappear. "Lost things have a habit of turning up," says Mr Spooner confidently.

They don't. Not always. Nana Anna lost a pair of glasses and they didn't turn up – mainly because she couldn't see to search for them properly.

Anyway, that was my school day and it was rubbish with a capital R – and now it's horrible with a capital H because Dolly-Rose is waiting for me for at the school gate.

"Did you tell someone that my mum was a tiler? I told you she wasn't and I overheard Lee saying that my mum was. You told him."

"No," I reply. "Maybe Lee's parents contacted her to do some tiling. I don't know."

"Are you saying I'm lying?"

"I dunno. Why would you tell lies? If you say your dad is a nuclear scientist and your mum's a brain surgeon and not a tiler then that's okay. I mean, it's okay if she *is* a tiler too." I blink and hold my breath for second.

Dolly-Rose, her face furious, swings her school bag around and it hits me in the guts. Then she stomps off back towards the playground. My eyes follow her and I want to shout that she's heading the wrong way if she's going home, but I don't. Instead I duck behind a bush and watch as she casually loiters by the big tree with the hole in it. I keep watching as she glances around, looking this way and that. She opens her school bag and takes out a book and pretends to read it, and then double-checks that the coast is clear before reaching into the hidey-hole and pulling out something small and golden...something that isn't me daydreaming... something that looks suspiciously like my missing goblet.

Before I can shout at her, Mr Spooner appears behind me and bellows, "Playing hide-and-seek, are we? Come on, get off home."

When I glance back, Dolly-Rose is gone.

My Balloon Poem

"Dandelion Clocks"
by Mabel Mynt

Dandelion seeds fly up on the breeze
Grant me a wish, oh dandelion, please
That once on the rock my worries will go
And all will be fine, that much I know

My heart is pounding as I stand on the rock
And higher float the seeds of that dandelion clock
This way and that, they rise and they fall
They swim on the breeze, like cotton wool balls

Up, up and away, for ever they go
Tiny speckles of white, like fresh winter snow
And I watch and I wish as onwards they fly
And to all of my worries, I wish you goodbye...

THE WALLED HEART

That evening I get the urge to go downstairs and out into the back garden to stare up at the sky. My feet patter across the damp grass and I smell wet earth and mouldy leaves and then I stop and glance upwards.

I feel tiny and alone like the smallest tadpole in the biggest ocean and even though I know Mum and Topaz are only two steps away from me I miss having Gavin around. I'm worrying about Mum so much that I can hardly think straight. Everything is going wrong and I'm at the centre of it all. I'm even worrying that I've lost the Goblet of Truth.

There's a hand on my shoulder and I spin around,

half-expecting a telling-off from Mum for being in the back garden and leaving the door open to let all the heat out. But it's Topaz. She looks at me and doesn't say a word and I don't think she even needs to. Instead we both look up at the sky and we don't talk but we both know we're there for each other.

A few minutes later I look at Topaz and I say, "I'm sorry."

"Don't be," replies Topaz. "You can't help being annoying."

When I've stopped pretend-belly-laughing I say, "You don't even know what I'm sorry for."

"It doesn't matter," Topaz fires back. "We've got to stick together, right?"

"Yes," I reply.

"And I'm here for you..."

"You mean you'd listen to anything I wanted to chat about?" I think about the worry suitcase and it's on the tip of my tongue to tell her.

"I wouldn't go that far," snorts Terrible Topaz and all the words I wanted to say disappear like sandcastles beneath the waves. A tiny voice inside me wonders if Topaz would laugh if I mentioned the suitcase. Maybe she wouldn't understand, just like number four on the list where I worry that I have a worry suitcase and I can't speak to anyone about it because no one would understand. "Ah, okay then. I suppose you can tell me anything. And...um...I could tell you anything?" Topaz pauses, serious now, and tucks a strand of hair behind her ear. "I mean, you'd listen to me? No matter what I said?"

I grunt, because I'm not sure I'd want to hear it.

After a second, Topaz says, "Well, even if you don't listen to me, you can still tell me stuff."

I feel a bit better, even though I've decided I won't say anything about the suitcase right now because no one will understand, even Topaz. "Can you see Saturn?" I say, pointing to the sky. "I'm always looking for it – sometimes it takes me so long to find it, I wonder if it's gone for ever." I think of Dad, wondering if he's gone for ever too. My heart hammers my ribs so hard it feels like a bird trying to escape a cage.

Topaz thinks about this but doesn't reply, instead I feel her arm hook into mine.

"I don't want things to be gone for ever," I whisper, my mind straying back to the last time I saw Dad. The image is sort of blurry now, like it happened so long ago it's just a collection of little snapshots. Bit by bit they flutter away until I'm thinking of Gavin and I realize I'm missing him as much as Dad, and maybe that's wrong.

I think about our chats about the stars and the SKYVIEWER 2020 and the amazing constellation light and the trip to the observatory, where I was happy when the man thought we were a family.

Topaz blows out tiny white balloons of breath as I ask her if she likes cheese strings or strawberry laces most. Before she answers, Mum shouts at us both to come inside because there's a terrible draught.

"You'll be frozen standing out there looking at the sky," Mum says, appearing at the back door and bundling us inside into the warm.

The living room is cosy and Mum has switched on the electric fire and we all sit on the sofa, Mum in the middle with me and Topaz on either side. And although it's lovely, it feels like Gavin should be in the kitchen, making tea and shouting out his stories about the galaxy. Mum ruffles Topaz's hair and then mine and Topaz tells Mum to be careful because she's just spent fifteen minutes trying to plait hers.

"I was looking at the stars," I tell Mum.

Mum swallows and says that's nice. But I know she's missing Gavin too. Her mobile phone has been silent for ages and we haven't had takeaway pizza since Gavin was here and I'm still feeling sad.

"I want to tell you something," whispers Mum. Topaz's eyes widen. Mum continues, "I wanted to say this before, about what happened with Gavin. You see, sometimes our hearts get broken once and we build a protective wall around ourselves. The thought of being hurt a second time is too much to bear. Maybe we see things differently because of it and maybe we are quicker to judge or to walk away so we can't be hurt again." Mum shrugs. "I don't want your hearts to get broken by him either, so I've texted Gavin and he's not coming back." She winces slightly and then pulls us both tighter into her body. I can smell Mum's skin, warm and sweet like fudge. "You girls are my priority. I don't want you caught up in drama. I try to protect you, you know. That's all I've ever done, rightly or wrongly."

"He's gone for good then," says Topaz, trying to hide her delight.

"I'm sad," I whisper.

"I know," replies Mum and I can tell she's sad too and although she's dumped him I don't think she wanted to, not deep down. "It *is* sad, but our hearts are very special and I don't want them broken by someone. We're the unit. We're the ones who need to stick together."

"Did Gavin break your heart, Mum?" I feel my shoulders droop.

Mum smiles but it doesn't reach her eyes. "Don't worry, Mabel. My heart had a wall around it anyway. My heart is fine."

But Mum's heart isn't fine. I know that and I'm worrying about it. What if Mum's not telling us that actually her heart has been smashed into tiny pieces like honeycomb bashed by a hammer? Mum eases herself out from between us and says we'll have fish fingers and chips for dinner. "Let's push the boat out," she says. Her eyes look sad, like a puppy dog who has just been told it can't go for walkies, ever.

I hate seeing Mum like this. I chew on the inside of my lip. From tomorrow I'm going to make things better because the goblet proved that Gavin was telling the truth. I'm determined to clear his name – as well as make things better for Mum.

The next day I start off in a positive mood, thinking I can make everything right. Positivity can change the world, according to Mr Spooner. So, I'm thinking positive.

For starters, Topaz is complaining that she doesn't

feel well enough to go to school and Mum checks her forehead and says it doesn't seem like she has a temperature. To be extra helpful and positive, I tell Mum that I'll make sure that Topaz gets to school safely, and if she's not well I'll report back. But Topaz, who glares at me, says she doesn't need my help. So, I tell her it's my duty to be a good sister.

Next, I tell Mum that she deserves a pampering day. I don't want her heart to be sad and it works, because Mum nods and her face lights up like fairy lights on a Christmas tree and she says that sounds like a sweet idea. I tell her we should go after school and pick up some things and then I'll give her a hand massage with some hand cream and paint her nails. For the first time in ages Mum gives me a big smile and says she'd enjoy that.

"What do you think you're doing?" spits Topaz as she slouches down the road.

"I'm doing good things," I tell her. "I don't want everyone to feel miserable."

"Well, keep your good things to yourself, because now I'm miserable that I have to go to school today."

Topaz chews on her nails and I tell her she needs a pampering session too. "Those nails are horrible, you've bitten them right down," I say. "And anyway, you don't look sick, so I don't see why you don't want to go to school. Think about all your friends – they'd miss you. Is this because of those girls we heard in the shop?"

Topaz snorts and then turns it into a cough. "I don't know what you mean."

"Why don't you feel like going to school then?"

"I told you, I feel ill. And stop sticking your nose in. I didn't even know those girls and that was ages ago and I haven't given it another thought. I've got so many friends that I can't be bothered worrying about some girls I don't even care about."

"Right."

"Right," replies Topaz.

Inside my head I'm thinking, *Wrong*. But what *is* wrong with Topaz?

"Mum's Broken Heart"

by Mabel Mynt

How do you mend a broken heart?
How do the pieces get taken apart?
Does it start life perfect as it can be?
And do bits fall off and then break free?

How do you understand a broken heart?
Does it ache, does it hurt, does it crack at the start?
I don't know how it works for others, you see
But Mum's sad and that's what worries me

I think that Mum's heart might be very sore
Might be squished, might be splintered, might have
dropped to the floor
For she is in love with a man who might be
A cheater, a loser, whose own heart runs free

And in this world what I want to be true
Is a happy heart for me and for you
And never more will our hearts start to crack
Because, Mum, I love you, and I've got your back

THE GOBLET RETURNS

After school, Mum is waiting in the car and toots the horn. She says Topaz texted that she didn't want to come to the shops and so she's going home by herself.

"I thought she'd jump at the chance to come into town," adds Mum. "I'd even considered getting her earrings, since I've stopped being annoyed about that. I don't know what's wrong with her. She seems so moody at the moment and she did say she didn't feel well this morning."

Mum starts the car and we drive to the nearest department store, where we're going to pick up stuff for the pampering session we're having later. Inside the store, we buy a hand cream that smells of roses and Mum tells me I can pick a nail polish for myself and one for Topaz, as maybe that will cheer her up. I pick purple glitter for Topaz and blue for me. Mum chooses a colour that looks the same as her fingernails, which is quite useless. But she says she prefers her nails to look natural.

I point out some perfume on a stand and Mum sprays it on herself.

"Ugh, it's like disinfectant," she exclaims, wafting her arms.

As we're walking away, something terrible happens. We spy Gavin and he's not alone. He's hugging Blonde Ponytail Woman and I sense Mum freeze to the spot when she sees them. I can't think of any words – all I can think about is Mum's heart smashing to smithereens. Gavin pulls out of the hug and Blonde Ponytail Woman takes his hand and brings it to her bump.

"He's feeling the baby kick," whispers Mum, her face the colour of putty.

"Oh," I say. Just oh.

Somehow, I feel like we shouldn't be here – like we're watching something we're not supposed to be watching. The worry suitcase feels so heavy that my knees almost buckle. Mum turns to me and gives me a brave smile and says it's been lovely, but maybe it's time we were going home. We don't walk past Gavin and Blonde Ponytail Woman. Instead we slope off in the opposite direction past the face creams and it doesn't help when a woman steps forward and tries to show Mum an anti-ageing cream, and Mum is saying she doesn't need it and the woman is explaining how you can combat frown lines.

"Frown lines," grimaces Mum, as we reach the car. She jumps in and pulls her seat belt across her. "The cheek! I don't have frown lines."

"Mum," I whisper. "I have this suitcase."

"Frown lines, indeed," seethes Mum. "There's nothing wrong with this face. It's as smooth as a baby's bottom. Somebody said the other day that I don't look a day over forty." That doesn't sound like much of a compliment when Mum's thirty-nine. "Sorry, I interrupted you." Mum swings the car around a corner. "What were you talking about?"

"Nothing." I stare out the window.

When we get home, I give Mum a hand massage with the cream and paint her nails, and although she smiles and says it's lovely, it's like her mind is somewhere else. "I remember being pregnant," she whispers. "It's a special time. Your dad used to always feel my bump when I was pregnant with you. He'd say 'I love you' to my belly."

I swallow. It's the first time Mum has mentioned Dad in ages and I know it's because she's thinking about what happened earlier with Gavin.

"We were happy," says Mum, staring at her nails. "In those days." Suddenly, her eyes cloud over like rain on a sunny day. "Anyway, that was a long time ago and a lot has changed since then, eh? Right, it's time to make some dinner. Thank you for the pampering session. It's cheered me right up."

I know it hasn't, because Mum's face is still sad no matter what she says.

Topaz isn't impressed with purple glittery nail polish either. When I go into her room to give it to her, she's face-planted on her bed. She looks up and then flops straight back down again, mumbling that I should go away. As I leave the nail polish on her bedside table and head back to the door, I think I hear her mutter, "I wish everything would float away like dandelion seeds on the breeze," – just like in the old story Dad used to tell us. And as I close the door, I'm certain I hear her crying.

The next day, I am planning to try something else

positive that will make everything right, because there is too much sadness in my house at the moment. Meanwhile, Mr Spooner definitely isn't sad. In fact, he's grinning like a happy squid as he waves us into the classroom, saying, "Okay, I have picked a winner for the poetry competition."

We all take our seats and Mr Spooner sets a jar of sweets on his desk and tells us he was thrilled with the level of work on the poems. "Each and every poem was special. I know you can't all be winners of the sweets, but you are all winners to me. You grasped the nettle."

Lee puts his hand up. "Sir, I didn't grasp any nettles."

"It's a saying," says Mr Spooner. "You took the bit between your teeth."

Lee is about say he didn't take anything between his teeth but Mr Spooner forges on. "Anyway, I am impressed by the standard. Your poems were exactly what I asked for – emotional. They were heartfelt. Except I wasn't so sure about the one about a dead bluebottle." Mr Spooner glances at Lee, who is grinning. "But I do appreciate that the poet wrote about how it feels to be squashed under a copy of a superhero comic. I wasn't sure we needed to list all the superheroes though or actually attach a squashed bluebottle, but again, I'm allowing for artistic interpretation."

"Did it win?" shouts Lee.

"No." Mr Spooner looks at his list and then touches the lid of the jar on his desk. I wonder if this is my moment, because I've been writing poems in my notebook at home for a while now, so I think I'm quite good at it. I've had a lot of practice. Mr Spooner picks up the jar and holds it aloft and says he knows we'd all love the sweets but he has a name in mind. "The winner has worked magic on her poem."

Her. Mr Spooner said *her*. That rules out all the boys. There's a groan, but only because they're not getting the sweets. Mr Spooner goes on to say that the poem was heartfelt and warm and he could tell the poet has a sweet heart. It's totally me. That's got to be about my "Dandelion Clocks" poem. I'm almost up off my seat as he announces, "The winner is..." I feel myself begin to shift. "Dolly-Rose, for her wonderful poem about her dog." I feel myself flop down. Dolly-Rose! A sweet heart! Her? Mr Spooner has got that wrong, because she thinks her dog isn't very nice. That's not someone with a heart!

"Sir," I say, hoisting my hand up. "Are you sure?"

"Yes, I'm certain," says Mr Spooner, smiling. He beckons Dolly-Rose up and she trots to the front of the room and takes the giant jar of sweets and says she's grateful to win such an important prize and this is the beginning of her being a star. It's like she's giving us an Oscar speech. She thanks her mum and dad and her nan and grandad and herself. I'm seething, thinking that Dolly-Rose didn't deserve to win the sweets for her poem about her dog. When she sits back down I lean over and say she didn't win the sweets fair and square. "You don't even have a pet, because you've told me so," I hiss. "Maybe you don't even live in a big house."

"Yes, I *did* live in a big house," Dolly-Rose says, looking around at everyone in the class. Her eyes are wide and I can see her hands trembling slightly. There's an audience now and Dolly-Rose is shaking her head, her plaits bouncing from side to side like a skipping rope.

"And your mum's not a brain surgeon. And you stole my goblet for yourself. I saw it in the tree. I bet you put it in your school bag after that. Sir." I wave my arms around. "Dolly-Rose took my goblet. It went missing, remember? It was in the classroom and Dolly-Rose took it. I think she put it in a tree and then in her school bag. Sir, I think we should look in her school bag."

"In a tree?" Mr Spooner raises one eyebrow.

"It's not in my school bag. You can look." Dolly-Rose chews on her lip.

Mr Spooner frowns at me, then he pulls open his drawer and pulls out my goblet. "I found it on the floor, Mabel. I think it must have fallen when we all rushed out for the fire drill. I put it in my drawer for safekeeping and was going to give it back to you yesterday but I completely forgot. I don't think it was ever hidden in a tree, but you have a good imagination."

"Oh," I mumble quietly and Mr Spooner tuts at me and shakes his head and says he expects more of me. When he gives me the goblet I shove it back in my blazer pocket and he tells us all to go out into the playground for break and to behave ourselves. On the way out I tell Dolly-Rose that I know she did it. I saw her by the tree. Dolly-Rose blinks and, for a brief second, I swear it looks like she's got a worry suitcase too.

ROOM TWENTY,
CASE TEN

My chance to make everything better and clear Gavin's name is a-go-go. I have been considering this most of the day, thinking that Gavin must have been telling the truth just like the goblet proved.

After school I text Mum and tell her I'm staying at homework club and she texts back to say she has let Topaz know not to meet me from school. And even though there was no reply she's sure Topaz will pick up the message. Mum also says she's going to be working a late shift at Fudge Fudge Wink Wink so I'm to go home after homework club and Topaz will pop a meal in the microwave for us both. I text back *okay* and then I go off on a mission to make everything right again.

I hurry towards Yes Lets, but I can see through the window that Gavin isn't in his usual seat. Quickly I swing open the door and the man me and Topaz saw here before looks up. He recognizes me and says he doesn't want me back asking questions about rings or where Gavin lives. I tell him it's Gavin I'm looking for.

"He has the day off," replies the man and then I hear him say if I want to leave a name he'll pass on a message, but I don't answer because I'm already too busy running.

Gavin isn't at his house either. I've rung the doorbell for ages but there isn't anyone there. That's when I remember something Gavin said. He said if anyone was looking for him they'd always find him at the observatory. He laughed like it was a joke, but that's where I need to go. I've got to ask him why he was giving someone a ring and patting their bump. I don't want my mum to have a wall around her heart. I want my mum's heart to be happy.

As I rush down the road, I pull out the golden goblet and stare at it, whispering, "Right, Mr Goblet. You've got two more truths to go and then I want you to work some magic on Mum's broken heart. Understand?"

To be honest, the Goblet of Truth doesn't answer. But I didn't expect it to anyway.

The observatory is open and I hurry through the door and up the steps and I wave at the man at the desk and say it's an emergency and I need to find Gavin. It's obvious he's confused and asks who I mean. "Gavin Bickerstaff," I add. "I need to find him quickly."

It's as though a light bulb has switched on inside his head as he echoes, "Gavin Bickerstaff." He touches his nose knowingly, then he tells me to go to the exhibition rooms on the right but I can't stay long because he's not supposed to let me in without paying. I promise him I'm not there to look at the exhibits, only he pulls a puzzled face.

Gavin isn't in the first exhibition room so I start looking in all the other rooms – rooms that we didn't get time to go into when we last visited the observatory.

There is a room with videos playing on the wall and I rush through it, Mars reflected in my face. Gavin's not in this room, or the next. There are glass cases full of tiny models of space stations and rockets and there is a whole area that looks like the surface of the moon with a flag on it. It's roped off so you can't walk on the moon yourself.

The next room is dark and you can hear bangs and

explosions and learn about stars being born and dying. Above me, chandeliers dangle from the ceiling, dripping with crystal droplets that look like stars. Straight ahead are heavy velvet curtains the colour of aubergines. The room smells like old musty books and forgotten antiques and a woman in a white blouse and navy-blue skirt stands at the door like she's a sentry. I don't see Gavin anywhere and I stop in front of the woman and say I'm trying to find him.

"Gavin?"

"Yes, Gavin Bickerstaff," I say. "He said he was always here."

The woman mulls this over for a second and then nods. "Ah, yes. Gavin. I know who you mean now. He's in room twenty. It's down the corridor. At the end of the room, case ten."

Case ten? I have no idea what the woman is talking about but I thank her and race down the dark corridor, my feet tapping on the tiles. I reach room twenty and run inside. The room is dim and empty. Gavin's not here – the woman was wrong. But she seemed so sure. I wander past a glass case full of items you'd find in a rocket and then past another. I pass case after case until I get to case ten and that's when my eyes are drawn inside.

There's a photograph of a woman and two children. The boy has a helmet of blond hair and is wearing shorts and his right knee has a plaster on it. The girl has a blonde ponytail and isn't looking at the camera but frowning at someone out of shot. The woman is smiling though, and wearing a flowery shirt and a plain skirt, and in her outstretched hand she's holding a piece of rock. The plaque underneath reads:

LOCAL DÓCHAS ASTRONOMER, PATRICIA CARINA WHEELER (PICTURED HERE WITH HER SON, GAVIN BICKERSTAFF, AND HIS TWIN SISTER, KATIE) FOUND A METEORITE IN JULY 1988. THE METEORITE WAS BROKEN INTO THREE PARTS. TWO BELONG TO MS WHEELER AND THE THIRD SHE GIFTED TO US AT THE DÓCHAS MUSEUM. THE MUCH LOVED LOCAL ASTRONOMER WORKED AT THE DÓCHAS OBSERVATORY FOR MANY YEARS AND WROTE A BOOK CALLED I NEED SPACE. THE BOOK WAS A SOURCE OF INSPIRATION TO GENERATIONS OF FUTURE ASTRONOMERS, INCLUDING PATIENCE GAMBO, WHO SAID, "PATRICIA WHEELER BROUGHT THE NIGHT SKIES ALIVE FOR ME AND MANY OTHERS.

I BELIEVE SHE HAS CREATED A NEW GENERATION OF ASTRONOMERS."

Patricia Carina Wheeler and her son Gavin Bickerstaff and his twin sister Katie! P. C. Wheeler! And the necklace Gavin was wearing had his *mother's* name on it, because her middle name is Carina. The woman at the observatory was right when she said Gavin was in case ten. He is. And Gavin said he could always be found at the observatory and he can – just not the way I thought he meant. He was telling us he was in an exhibit with his mother, because she's P. C. Wheeler and an important astronomer. No wonder he was smiling and winked when he said it. And when we were in the observatory the last time, Patience Gambo said there was a VIP in the audience. It must have been Gavin! She knew he was there. Only he went to the toilet and didn't hear what she said. My head feels like it's about to explode. But why didn't Gavin say his mother wrote the book when I showed it to him? I don't understand. And why doesn't he ever talk about her much?

When I get home there's a package on the floor of the hall. The postman must have delivered it through the letter box after Mum left for Fudge Fudge Wink Wink. It's addressed to me so I carefully tear open the edge. Underneath the brown wrapping paper is a signed copy of *I Need Space* by Patricia Carina Wheeler. When I open the front page I see a small note and I read it slowly:

Dear Mabel,

I'm not very good at writing letters but I thought you'd like this gift. It will probably be my last gift to you as your mum and I have decided to part. I know this is your favourite book and I know you can no longer buy it. This one is a signed copy I had at home. The thing is, I thought about giving you this before, but I didn't want you to think that I was trying to take anything away from your dad, as he gave you your original copy. He's special and his place in your heart will never change. I understand this and I wouldn't ever dream of trying to be your dad when you already have one. But I hope we're friends. Good enough for me to send this to you.

I also want to tell you that I've been keeping a secret though perhaps not the sort of secret you've been imagining – Patricia Carina (the name on my necklace) Wheeler is my mother and she wrote the book before she married my dad. I know you love her work and I should have talked more about her to you all, but I wasn't ready. You see, my mother is a very private person and hasn't been well recently. I've been visiting her on Tuesdays, as I said. But please enjoy the book, as my mother would be very happy to know how much you love it and the stars.

Love Gavin. X

PS The SKYVIEWER 2020 was given to me by my mother and it was her favourite telescope. I hope when you look through it you feel connected to the stars. We are all made of stardust, after all, just as my mum once said.

I run upstairs and put the book on my shelf and shout to Topaz, because I want to explain to her what I've been told about Gavin and his mum and his necklace being nothing to do with Blonde Ponytail Woman.

No one answers back.

The house feels empty and I guess Topaz must be on

her way home from school and be a bit late, so I send her a text saying: TOPAZ, you'll never guess what!!!! I have something to tell you. You won't believe what I've been told. Where are you? I put my usual world, sun, moon and stars emojis at the end and hit send.

There's a bleep from Topaz's bedroom. The door is partly open and I go inside and there's all this stuff on her bed that I don't recognize: earrings, hairclips, jewellery, a box of DIY friendship bracelets – and in the middle sits her phone. Usually Topaz has it with her. I know I shouldn't, but I check to see if she's got any messages or if she's texted anyone to say she's going round to their house. After all, Topaz has millions of friends. There is the text from me and the earlier text from Mum saying that I'm at homework club and she's to put a meal in the microwave for us later. But there are no texts from anyone else, and when I check her contacts there aren't any. It's like Topaz has wiped away all her friends. Or worse still, like she has no friends.

My heart skips a beat.

It doesn't make sense.

Topaz is nowhere in the house. I know because I've checked everywhere. I even looked under my bed until

Jupiter hissed me a warning to leave him alone. I feel the weight of the worry suitcase and each breath I take feels sharp and jagged. There are about one million thoughts running through my head but the main one is I'VE GOT TO FIND TOPAZ. I feel like I'm losing everyone I care about. Within seconds, I'm putting my school blazer on again and I grab an umbrella and run down Bristo Road, my feet battering puddles of rain on the pavement.

The lights are still on in Topaz's school and I hang around the school gates for ages, hoping that she's doing something after school that she forgot to mention. That's when I see some girls who I think might be in her class, and they look like the same girls we saw on the bus and in the shop. I stop them as they come through the gates and I ask them if Topaz is still in school.

One of them looks at me blankly and the other girl says, "Topaz. The one with a secret. You know..." I recognize her voice immediately from the shop. She takes some gum from her pocket and puts it in her mouth and chews.

I mumble that I don't think Topaz has secrets and the girl shrugs and says Topaz hasn't been in class today at all, so she must be sick. They laugh, nudge each other and walk on.

"I think she overheard us," mumbles one of the girls as they walk away from me. "In the toilets. Bet that's why she didn't come in today." They laugh again and disappear down the road.

"Not in school," I mumble, my heart tripping. How could Topaz not have been in school all day? How come no one noticed that? And how come Topaz has been lying about having friends and biting her nails so much recently, like she's nervous? I know she did go to school this morning because we walked half the way there together. I glare at the girls, my eyes like daggers. They're being horrible to Topaz.

If only I knew why.

DANDELION SEEDS ON THE BREEZE

I'm not a good sister. I've been too busy worrying about everything except Topaz. And now I am worried about her. She's been in such a bad mood recently that I've found it difficult to talk to her. I'd go to say things and then hold them back. I'd try to ignore the things I felt in my gut and swallow back all my fears about our mixed-up, muddled-up life. But thinking back to that night when we looked at the stars, she asked if she could tell me anything and I didn't answer. So she never told me what was on her mind and that was my fault.

I cross my fingers, hoping that if I think hard I'll realize where Topaz is and why she hasn't been at school. Only Topaz doesn't seem to be anywhere in the town – she's not hanging around the chip shop or Bread Pitt; she's not on the swings in the park or outside the estate agency. She's not anywhere I can think of. I wonder if Topaz would have gone back to Gavin's or even to The Fir Trees. I'm so desperate now that I'm retracing all our steps and visiting all the places we've been to recently.

She's not at Gavin's. Gavin isn't even at Gavin's. The house is still empty and I ring the doorbell for ages. A neighbour comes out and says Gavin isn't in and maybe he's at the hospital. "That baby must be due any day," she shouts as I run down the road.

When I ring the doorbell at The Fir Trees the same woman as before opens it and looks at me while fat raindrops fall off my umbrella. "Is Topaz here?" The woman shakes her head and says she doesn't know anyone by the name of Topaz. That's when I say, "Does Patricia Carina Wheeler live here?" The woman says "yes" and asks if I'm family. "Almost," I reply. She looks at me and says "almost" isn't enough for me to visit her.

"And even if I let you in, I'm not sure she'd necessarily remember you from her past," the woman says softly.

"Gavin comes and visits her..." I whisper, feeling the

276

colour drain from my face. "This is a care home for old people, isn't it?"

"Yes, and yes." The woman pauses and then inhales. "He visits every Tuesday with his twin sister, Katie. She's having a baby any day now, but she never misses a visit. She's a sweetie, that one."

"So that must mean Katie is Blonde Ponytail Woman," I realize, talking more to myself than the woman.

"Who?" The woman looks confused. "If you're asking me if Katie has a blonde ponytail, then yes, she does. But I'm afraid I don't have time for this."

"I need to speak to Gavin right now – it's urgent. I need his help," I say, but the woman tells me he's not here. "I've lost Topaz," I whisper. "And I've lost Gavin. I'm so worried."

"Lost him?" the woman says, staring at me. "Whatever makes you think that? Anyway, he'll come back."

"I lost my dad too," I say, turning and running down the path. "And he is never coming back. So why should anyone else?"

The sky is as dark as Jupiter's coat and rain is falling like tiny arrows. A gust of wind grabs the umbrella from my fingers and it flies off down the road like a broken-winged bat. But I don't care if I get wet because I'm more worried about Topaz. I feel my heart batter in my chest and I'm dragging the world's biggest worry suitcase with me as I rush down the streets. What if I deserve the suitcase and I don't realize? No one else seems to have a suitcase like mine, so I must have done something wrong to have to keep lugging around all these worries.

My feet pound the pavements as the rain soaks my uniform and splashes up my grey socks, leaving large splodges shaped like teardrops. Angry flashes turn the world negative and a massive rip of thunder tears the sky apart. The air is heavy like clotted cream and I try to inhale but it catches in my throat and I realize I need to get to Topaz more than I've ever needed anything before. Trees blur as I run around the edge of the lough and bruised clouds weep above me.

Topaz has disappeared and I can't let it be for good.

My mind is racing like a horse in full gallop, over all the things we've said and all the places we've been recently. That's when I remember how Topaz was lying on her bed and I swear she muttered that she wished everything could float away like dandelion seeds on the breeze. Dad used to say that too. Topaz hadn't mentioned it for the longest time though and then recently she's mentioned it twice. I wonder if it's important now. It's a long shot, but it's the last place I can think of that Topaz might come.

The lough is spilling over as I race past it, zigzagging this way and that and shouting Topaz's name. I run through brambles and past the fuchsia bushes that Dad used to say were God's teardrops. My own teardrops are falling fast.

"You've lost her, stupid!" I yell. "Stick that in the worry suitcase and carry it for ever. Everyone's leaving and all you'll be left with is the stupid suitcase. Dad's gone, Topaz has gone. And Gavin's gone too. Everyone's gone." I run faster, heading towards the wild hills behind the lough. I feel defeated and I can hardly figure out what to do. "You don't pay enough attention to everyone," I rant at myself. "You tried to put things right but it was too late. Topaz needed you and you didn't notice." My feet pound up the hill, past rocks and stones, along the twisting pathways, higher and higher.

The shouty voice in my head chases me as I run onwards. The stones are slippery and I keep losing my footing and stumbling. But I run on. Below, I see Dóchas and the lough and I'm running and falling over skiddy rocks and I'm screaming for Topaz and just when I think everything's crumbled and my legs are too weak to go on – when there's a tidal wave of sorrow inside me, rising, falling, breaking over the suitcase – I stop, not knowing what else to do but scream Topaz's name. It comes out loud, raw and sharp, as though it's straight from my heart. The word bursts through the night sky: "TOPAZ…"

There's a rumble of thunder and the rain lashes against my body, sharp like tiny pencil points poking me. "Don't go, Topaz," I bellow. "You can't leave like Dad did." And then I howl, like I've never done before. "There's no one to fist-bump and no one to say 'I love you' with and no one to tell me about romance books or laugh at silly jokes but then end up arguing with me because we always do." I scream Topaz's name again, louder and longer this time.

In the distance I hear a muffled voice and it sounds like Topaz yelling back at me. I call her name again and the voice bellows: "Yes, I'm here. I'm at Dóchas Rock."

I turn and ascend higher, gasping as I weave my way to find her. As I reach the summit of the rock, the sky roars and birds scatter. I stop when I see Topaz. She rushes towards me and gives me a hug and it's like hugging a giant sodden sponge. "What's wrong with you?" I yell over the thunder. "Why weren't you at school today and why are you here? I thought you'd run away from me. I don't want to lose you!"

Topaz looks at me, confused. "I didn't run away from you!" she yells back.

All my words come out in a tumble. "If it's about Gavin then we made a mistake. He's not like the man in your romance books. And Mum isn't Summer." I explain what I think I know and how we didn't give him a chance. "We didn't give ourselves a chance either," I shout at her over the rain. "We're not living inside one of your books. It's not a love triangle. Gavin loves Mum. And Mum loves Gavin. I don't want Mum to have a wall around her heart. I don't want us to have walls around ours."

Topaz shakes her head. "I don't care about those stupid books. And I didn't come here because of Galactic Gavin." A whip-crack of lightning flashes across the sky, illuminating her face. "I didn't know where else to go. I came here because of Dad."

"And the story about worries floating away on the breeze, like dandelion seeds?" I blink, rain streaming down my face.

"Yes," Topaz replies. "I remembered the story. The one he once told us at the picnic and the story he told you every bedtime. Well, I want Dad to float away, because he's not the dad we thought he was."

I swallow, confused. "This is about *Dad* floating away?"

Topaz's eyes grow dark like stormy clouds. "They know about Dad. They didn't like me before and things were hard at my new school, but now they know what Dad did and it's worse than ever. They aren't nice to me."

"They?" I shake my head.

"The girls at school. They know...they know where he is. They know a secret that we didn't know."

I'm not sure what secret Topaz is talking about and rainwater dribbles down my face as it scrunches in confusion. "But how could they know where Dad is when we don't know where he is and neither does Mum?"

"She *does* know," spits Topaz. "She always knew. Mum knows exactly where Dad is and she didn't tell us."

I think back to the envelope and Mum lying. And it hurts like a paper cut to the heart.

I blink.

I blink again.

Again.

I feel like I blink dozens of times in one go.

"Dad did go away." Topaz's eyes are steely-cold now.

I feel my lips mumble, "But why...?" If Mum knows where Dad is, then why didn't she tell us? Why didn't we go and see him? Why didn't he come and see us?

"I'll tell you why!" yells Topaz.

I blink.

"He's in prison, that's why. And I know because of a girl in my class. Her mum works nearby and she saw our mum going into the prison. And then she recognized Mum from the coffee morning at my school and put two and two together."

I stop mid-blink and the world stops with me. I barely hear Topaz explain that's why those girls were talking about her – they'd judged her without knowing her at all. Those girls didn't like her to start with and they thought this proved why they shouldn't. And we didn't know a thing about it. "He was convicted of stealing, Mabel. I looked him up on the internet and there was an article about him in the local paper. It made me feel terrible. But it's worse than that." Topaz's voice drops. "I've been stealing too. I took money from Mum's purse. The money she noticed was missing. I only wanted to borrow it. I wanted to fit in with everyone at school. I wanted to be just like everyone else. But it didn't work. I didn't fit in and now I know I'm just as bad as Dad. He's in prison, Mabel. Did you hear me?"

"You're lying, Topaz Mynt. You're lying."

Topaz looks at me and then bites on her bottom lip. I look up at Topaz, my eyes filling with tears. I think about pulling the golden goblet from my pocket, but I don't because I realize Topaz *is* telling me the truth. I can tell by looking in her eyes. And in my head, I see a crack healing in the goblet until there's only one final crack left.

Topaz has told me the truth. I know it.

And then I realize I don't care about the cracks in the stupid goblet now anyway, because my heart has just cracked into so many pieces it's like shattered sugar. I feel a numbness spread to every part of me, like ice spreading across a frozen pond. The worries feel so heavy that I'm catching my breath. My chest rises and falls. I turn and move closer towards the edge of the rock, trying to find somewhere I can breathe easier, but it feels like I'm dragging the suitcase with me. It's too heavy now, worse than it's ever been. I feel bits of worries begin to spill out as I whimper. I think of the contents flying into the air – worries and problems flying everywhere, blinding me.

Dóchas Rock is where Dad said my worries would float away on the breeze. This is the exact spot. So, I stand on top of the jagged rock, my toes gripping the edge, and I scream that I don't want the worry suitcase. And I feel the weight of it on me and I try to lift all my worries up and away but they're so heavy I can't bear it.

My eyes flood with tears and I can hear Topaz yelling at me to come away from the edge and saying she's sorry but it was the truth and she had to tell me and I'm to be careful I don't slip. My worries are supposed to float away now, that's what Dad said. But the imaginary suitcase feels harder and harder to lift and the worries are so lumpen and heavy that I feel them deep inside my soul...and that's when I close my eyes, hoping the suitcase and all my worries will just disappear. Only I lose my footing on the slippery rock and then my ankle jolts and I feel myself fall forwards.

My arms begin spinning around like windmills.

Maybe it would look funny in slow motion.

Only this feels like it's been speeded up.

It doesn't feel like me falling.

Only it is.

My heart flutters.

The air doesn't support me, but Dad is right – as I fall, I feel my worries floating away, until there's a dull thud and everything goes black. The worry suitcase is forgotten. Everything is.

I

see

stars

THE DARKNESS

When the stars explode it feels like I'm left surrounded by a huge black cloak. Like it has covered my head with a blanket of darkness and no matter how much I try to free myself, I can't. Worse still, I don't even know if I can move. And if I do, where would I go? I can't go to Dad, who told me to come to the rock.

Not Dad, who is somewhere else, not here with us.

A voice drifts alongside me, saying, "I've got to go." It sounds like Topaz but I can't be sure because it gets tangled up inside my head.

I am alone; light as a balloon, heavy as an elephant. My head feels like a broken doll that's been thrown to the floor and I imagine the worry suitcase scattered around me; worries landing here, there and everywhere like socks. Slowly I sink into the darkness, being enveloped by black as far-reaching as a black hole. Terror sweeps over me like a wave breaking over my body. Despite trying to fight it, I sense the darkness is stronger than me and I won't be able to defeat it.

Somewhere out there in the galaxy, Mum is serving chunks of fudge and Dad is sitting in a locked room, and they don't know I'm here. But I want them to know, because I don't like the darkness that has swept me up and I want to find my way back. Dad won't come to save me though. He can't. He can't get out.

I wish I was at home right now, fist-bumping him.

Bump, bump.

The words "I love you" die on my lips. Or maybe my lips didn't even move. I sense a flicker somewhere beyond the blackness. *You're imagining it,* I tell myself. No one is here. "I love you," I try to say again. *Can you be swallowed up by worry?* I know that I can. *Can you let the worries go?* I don't think so. The more I try to move, the more my head hurts. Then I sense another tiny movement, like a little pinprick of a star shimmering through the black cloak. *You are alone,* I tell myself. *Alone.*

"Mabel!" A voice in the distance splits the darkness. But it's far away and I'm here, parts of me scattered and my suitcase full of worries still surrounding me and it feels like it has crushed every part of my body. My breath comes in tiny sharp stutters and punctures the air like a stapler. Everything suddenly comes flooding back – the lies, the truths, Topaz stealing and my dad in prison. My head hurts – there's a tiny thudding at the back like there's a little man inside with a hammer and when I try to move he hammers harder.

"Mabel."

Footsteps grow as I lie, quiet and deflated, on a pile of rocks. Slowly I attempt to ease myself up on my elbows. I can hear voices and the puffing of someone above me. "I'm here," I whisper, my body drained by the weight I've been hauling around. "I'm here." The words slip into the storm and are carried away on the wind, rising into the night air, then scattering.

"Okay, you're speaking, thank goodness," Gavin is shouting. I can see the top of his head now as he leans over the edge of Dóchas Rock above me and then my eyes travel onwards to the sky, to billions of tiny stars, and it's like I'm in my perfect cloud-bed, staring at the pinpricks of light from the constellation light. "Mabel, you'll be okay." I focus and see Gavin's face again, shining through the darkness. Mum and Topaz are there too, peering over the rock, and Mum is shouting that I'll be fine and that Topaz had to leave me for a bit to get help because she'd left her mobile phone at home. Mum says I've just got to lie still and let Gavin climb down to see me and check me over and she's phoned for an ambulance – it's on its way. Gavin is struggling, climbing down the rocks now, his feet slipping in the wet, and I can hear Mum telling him to be careful because she doesn't want him to get hurt too. I close my eyes for a second and when I open them again Gavin is crouched beside me, his face full of concern.

"I was worried about you," he says, pushing a lock of wet hair from my forehead. "I thought you'd..." He pauses. Tiny flickers of fear ignite in his eyes. "I thought you'd really hurt yourself. You haven't fallen too far, only onto a lower ledge, but I think you might have bumped your head on the way down. You've been here for a little while before we could get to you. I was at the hospital when I got the message from your mum. She said she needed me, that you all needed me, and I came immediately."

I mumble something about being sorry and Gavin strokes my cheek and tells me everything's okay. He was at the hospital with his sister as she was having her baby, but he tells me not to worry about that because I'm very important to him too and his sister insisted he go.

I think of the suitcase. I am hurting – but inside where no one can see it. "I was trying to throw it away," I whisper. My eyes meet Gavin's.

Gavin takes my hand in his, which is warm against my frozen fingers. He says it won't be long until help comes and he takes off his coat and puts it over me like a blanket. "Topaz has explained what happened." Gavin doesn't let go of my hand and his eyes are searching mine and when I go to close my eyes he tells me to stay awake and that we should talk. He asks me what I'd like to talk about.

"The suitcase." I swallow. "I was trying to throw it away."

"The suitcase?" Gavin says he's happy to talk about suitcases if it'll keep me awake until help comes. He says he's got a suitcase and it's got wheels and there's a blue ribbon on the handle so that he knows it's his when he sees it amongst all the other suitcases. I tell him I don't need a ribbon to know mine, because it never leaves me.

"I worry that it'll never get lighter," I whisper. "That's on my list. And I worry that I can never get rid of the suitcase. I should have remembered that before I tried to throw it away."

"You tried to throw away a suitcase? When you fell?" Gavin looks around. "Where is it?"

"You can't see it but it's full," I mutter. "I've been carrying it around since Dad left and I've been putting all my worries in it and dragging it about. But now it's so heavy and I don't want it but I can't get rid of it. I've even been dreaming about it. Dad said my problems and worries would float away if I stood on the rock. But the worries didn't float away because the suitcase is still here."

Gavin squeezes my hand and maintains eye contact and I'm almost certain he can see the suitcase reflected in my eyes. "I'm sorry about your dad and the suitcase and I know that I can't change anything that's happened. But if the suitcase is too heavy for you, then come and talk to me and maybe we could lighten it. Is that what you mean?"

I try to speak but Gavin tells me not to use my energy up.

"I'm here for you, Mabel. We're all here for you and you don't have to carry that suitcase of worries alone – not when we can all help you. Not when maybe, just maybe, I could carry the suitcase for you for a while. If you want me to."

I feel a tear escape my eye and roll down the side of my head. "I want you to," I manage to whisper. "I'm tired." My eyes begin to close and Gavin squeezes my hand and says I need to look at him and I'm not allowed to fall asleep. My eyes flutter open again and I mumble, "I didn't know where my dad was and I know where he is now and it doesn't make things better. It just makes the suitcase heavier. It's another thing to add." My eyes are leaking more, tiny rivers mingling with rainwater. I tell Gavin that I love my dad and he's not a bad person because if he was bad maybe that would mean Topaz and me were bad too. Another tear follows. And then another, until my face is soaking wet.

"Of course you're not bad people, and I'm sure your dad isn't either," replies Gavin and he takes a tissue from his pocket and tries to wipe away rain and tears, and the tissue gets so wet that it falls apart in his hand. "I might not know your dad but I know both you and Topaz and you're incredible. I'm proud of you both. And I know you're a good, kind and sweet person, Mabel. It shines inside you like the brightest star. You know this rock above us? Do you know its name?"

I mumble that it's called Dóchas Rock and everyone knows that.

Gavin smiles and says, "Yes, that's the name. But it

means so much more."

"If you look beneath the surface?"

"Yes," replies Gavin. "Exactly. The name Dóchas means 'hope' and you've got that in bucket loads, Mabel. You're kind and caring and your heart is in the right place and that's way more important than any old suitcase. Always and for ever."

"Always and for ever?"

"Always and for ever. And remember I mentioned your mum said she needed me – that you all needed me? And I came straight here…" Gavin pauses. "What I didn't get a chance to say was that, just as much as you need me, I need you. I'd like to be part of your family."

The wind roars across us, making leaves rise up into a tiny tornado and then scatter, before rising again. As Gavin looks down at me he smiles and then he leans down and gives me a gentle hug, and he's warm and I feel the weight of the suitcase suddenly lighten and I can breathe properly for the first time in ages.

LET'S LIGHTEN ALL OUR SUITCASES... TOGETHER

Mum and Topaz are waiting by the ambulance and Mum is still in her Fudge Fudge Wink Wink pinafore and her face is creased with frown lines. She says that Topaz has told her everything and there is no need to worry any further.

I'm taken to the hospital with Mum, Gavin and Topaz. Then Gavin disappears for a while, saying he has to check on his sister as her baby is coming any time now. We sit until the doctor comes in to see me. He says that he's checked my tests and there is no damage done, except a bump to the head that happened when I fell. He says they'll keep me in overnight for observation but

I'm free to go home first thing in the morning as long as Mum is keeping an eye on me and I get plenty of rest and take a day or two off school. The doctor gives us a friendly salute and then leaves us to it, telling me to take care and no more climbing on rocks.

Topaz says she wishes she could take a few days off. I look at her and Mum looks at me and says that Topaz has told her everything. "I'm going to speak to the school," says Mum, putting her arm around Topaz and pulling her into a hug. "I should have told you everything about Dad sooner and I'm sorry I didn't realize secondary school was such a lonely place for you. But it will change, I'll make sure of it."

The next morning, when Gavin arrives to take us home he says his sister had a baby girl overnight. "I'm an uncle," he adds proudly. "So, I suppose I'll be looking after a baby in my spare time." Mum squeezes Gavin's arm and tells him to enjoy the nappy-changing, although I'm not sure "enjoy" is the right word.

When we return home, Mum says it's time to talk properly about everything that's been going on and Gavin says he should go. Topaz shakes her head and says we made a lot of mistakes about him and it's time to put them right.

"We thought you were cheating on Mum," explains

Topaz, her face blushing with embarrassment. "We saw you with a woman with a blonde ponytail and you had a ring and we thought she was Carina because you were wearing this necklace with the name on it and we discovered she had a necklace too. And then we saw she was pregnant and I put two and two together..."

"And got twenty-two?" asks Mum.

"And I had this romance book and Summer was being cheated on by Autumn and this man. And it was a love triangle. It convinced me your Blonde Ponytail Woman was Carina and she was like Autumn and Mum was Summer. And it was another triangle." Topaz glances at Gavin.

"I'm not sure what was going on in your book, but this Blonde Ponytail Woman you're talking about is Katie, my twin. She's been staying with me while her partner is away on business. I promised him I'd look after her. And Carina is my mother – Patricia Carina. Katie and I have matching necklaces with Mum's name on. I just got Katie's engraved for her as a present. It is important for us – we like to keep Mum close to our hearts." Gavin looks at Mum and shakes his head. "As for the ring," he whispers, "I'm sorry for all the confusion. Part of this is my fault. When the ring was brought up before I didn't explain it properly because there *was* a ring. So, you girls were right. I was hiding it and I lied, but not for a bad reason."

Mum's eyes widen.

Gavin turns to us. "It was a secret. I was showing Katie a ring I'd had made specially and I didn't want your mum to know. My sister tried it on and she said it was beautiful and she was so happy for me. We discussed it a few times because I wanted a woman's input. I'm not great with jewellery. I even told the guy at work about it because I was so thrilled about how amazing the ring had turned out, but everyone was sworn to secrecy." Gavin turns his gaze towards Mum. "I had it made for you. I lied when the girls mentioned it because I didn't think the time was right to give it to you. I wanted it to be special."

Mum's like liquid chocolate now – she's gone gooey and is melting all over Gavin's words.

"I will give it to you later and explain its significance. But I didn't talk about it at the time because it was a surprise."

Topaz mouths, "Ooops."

"And regarding my mum... Well, she is Mum and I love her and I didn't discuss her with you because I didn't think you needed to know, but I do visit her on Tuesdays, like I said, with Katie. She's in a care home called The Fir Trees because she has dementia. I love her very much." He looks at me and then dips his eyes. "I think I had a suitcase of worries for ages too, like yours, Mabel, and I didn't tell anyone how heavy they were. I carried my own suitcase around and didn't talk to you all about it. I thought they were my worries and I was alone with them. I wasn't sure anyone would understand. I am sorry."

I nod, tears threatening my eyes.

"But you're not on your own now, Gavin," says Mum, slipping her fingers into his. "I should have realized you weren't cheating. It was such a stupid thing to think." She rakes her fingers through her hair. "I built a wall round my heart after the girls' dad left." She looks at us and whispers, "I didn't ever want to get hurt again and I think I was a bit afraid. It might still take time for the wall to come down properly." Slowly, Mum's eyes begin to glimmer with tears. "And you should have told me more about your mum, Gav. I knew you were visiting her but you should have explained the whole story. I'd have understood. It's just that I've been preoccupied recently and maybe I had my own suitcase of worries too."

Eventually, Mum says Gavin mentioned the suitcase situation to her and she hopes I'm not annoyed that he told her. I shake my head, saying I don't mind. Topaz looks at me and then Mum and Gavin and she thinks for a second and then says she also had a suitcase of worries, but didn't know how to explain it either.

"I thought I was on my own with the worries," whispers Topaz. "Secondary school is harder than I thought. I tried to fit in with everyone in my class, by buying all the same things they had. I stole money from Mum's purse that morning I went back to pick up my lunch box. You were getting ready for the appointment, Mum. I took the money to pay for the things I wanted, and that makes me just as bad as Dad."

Mum shakes her head. "You may have taken the money and it was wrong, you know that. Dad may have taken money too and what he did was wrong. But I forgive you. You made a mistake and you're sorry. And I forgive Dad, because he made a mistake and I know he's sorry too. Everyone deserves a second chance, don't they? We all make mistakes but we're all allowed to move on. We can't stand still. Even the earth doesn't stand still."

Topaz whispers, "I'm sorry, Mum."

Mum manages a hoarse, "It's okay," back and squeezes her hand. "I was running away from everything and I skipped school. And I've done it once before."

I say, "I saw you, Topaz. You walked past our school one day. We were outside. I wanted to run to you but I couldn't. I wish I'd talked to you then."

"Everything felt like a huge weight on my shoulders," Topaz mutters. "I was worrying about school and not having any friends. I was worrying no one liked me. I wanted to fit in so much I did stupid things. That was my suitcase, wasn't it?"

I nod.

"I think, as a family, we don't need all these suitcases. So what if, like Gavin mentioned, we have a time where we can talk about the things that worry us. It seems like talking helps. 'A problem shared is a problem halved' sort of thing, no?" We nod at Mum. "Let's lighten all our suitcases together."

THE RUCKSACK

Mum's right, we should share our worries. And there's one that's been niggling inside my head that now pops straight out of my mouth without me feeling like I can't say it. "Does Dad still love us? That's the worry. We didn't fist-bump that night and we didn't say we loved each other and then he disappeared. I miss him." I search Mum's face for the truth.

She says that Dad still loves us and that she's sorry she didn't tell us all this. She said she thought about it for ages but she was trying to protect us. Then Mum says that nothing has changed in Dad's love and it never will, no matter where he is.

She sighs and adds, "Dad has always loved you and he always will. No walls can change that. I'm sorry he hasn't been here to fist-bump you or tell you he loves you. But be sure that he does."

"But I've got such a big space in my heart where Dad used to be," I add.

Mum touches my hair and pulls me in close.

Gavin goes to get up and Topaz grabs his wrist and pulls him back, telling him not to go. Only this time she doesn't call him Galactic – just Gavin.

"Mum," I say, pulling away. "Even if I've got a space where he should be, I still love Dad, no matter what."

Mum says she knows that and Dad knows too. "I have visited Dad in prison recently and we discussed this – how much he loves you both and how him leaving will have left a hole in your lives. He's also written to me and phoned." Mum squeezes my hand. "I didn't tell you I was in contact with him because I was waiting for the right time. But there never seemed to *be* a right time. I was worried how it would upset you. So I just said I had an appointment. The appointment was to see Dad."

Topaz looks at me. This explains why Mum was going out that morning dressed smartly, and the mysterious phone call. It was Dad on the other end of the line.

"It was hard seeing Dad in there," says Mum. "And, as you know, I even bumped into one of the mums from your school that day, Topaz. When she saw me at the coffee morning she recognized me and knew I'd been in the prison." Mum glances at Topaz, her face full of concern. "Then she must have told her daughter. I'm sorry you overheard what they said about Dad." She looks deflated like a burst balloon. "At the beginning, when Dad first went in, I didn't have the courage to go and visit him. I tried to bury the truth for ages, to not face what had happened. You could say I stuffed the whole thing in a suitcase of worries and carried it around with me, because I couldn't talk to anyone. It was hard and I tried to block it all out for a while. I avoided walking past the places Dad used to work. People avoided me too and pretended not to know Dad. Then the worries I had got heavier and heavier. But eventually I went to visit him, and when I saw Dad he said he was sorry and we started trying to figure out how best to tell you. I didn't want to rush it, but now I wish I'd told you sooner."

"I found out in the school toilets," whispers Topaz. "I was in a cubicle when they came in and I stayed hidden in there until they left, but they knew I was there. I think they did it on purpose. They laughed about Dad being in prison. I was left sitting on the toilet, crying."

"I should have known not to keep it from you. I was foolish. And I'm so, so sorry. I'm only human and I've made mistakes, ones I truly regret. I knew you would find out one day. But it should have come from me." Mum takes Topaz's hand and gives it a squeeze and then she takes mine and gives mine a squeeze too. Mum tells Topaz she should have gone into school yesterday though and she asks where she'd been all day in the cold. Topaz says she'd been sitting looking out over the lough, hoping all her problems would fly away. Only they didn't. They just got bigger.

"Okay," whispers Mum. "You know, that was just one of Dad's stories. He's good at telling stories. But problems don't magically fly away on the wind. Although perhaps they can be helped by sharing them."

According to Mum, I can write to Dad. We both can. Topaz says she's not good with words and she doesn't think she wants to write to him yet and Mum says that's okay – that no one is going to force her to make any decisions or to rush things. We can deal with it all in good time. Mum says we can visit Dad too, maybe one day in the future. Dad made a mistake doing what he did, stealing and selling the items on, but mistakes only stay with you if you don't do anything about them. Mum says Dad is doing something about it – he's going to change. Not change completely, because he's still our dad and that will remain the same. But he's not going to keep selling stuff he shouldn't be selling. He told Mum it was wrong and he was sorry to put us all through this. He's learned from his mistakes. Mum also explains that the other thing that has changed is them not being together any longer. As much as she cares for him, they won't be getting back together. Sometimes things don't always work out the way you expect and although some things change, what won't change is that Dad is important. He is part of our family and that makes him special and we will always respect that. Mum says she is happy that she met Dad all those years ago because it meant she had us and we mean the world to her and we're part of Dad too.

I'm in my bedroom, staring at the shattered goblet. It was in my pocket when I fell off Dóchas Rock and it broke completely when I landed. I know that Topaz told me the truth about Dad when we were up there, so by rights the goblet should only have had one crack left. The final truth. Instead there are lots of tiny pieces, which I throw in the bin. I feel myself whisper goodbye and I say a little prayer like Mum does when she buries a mouse or a bird (only Mum's prayer goes something like this: *Please, I pray I never have to clean up a dead animal again*). Jupiter stares into the bin and then licks his lips and walks away, which is exactly the same thing he does when Mum buries his "gifts".

As I push the bin under my dressing table, there's a knock on the door. It's Topaz and she comes in and sits on the bed beside me.

"You were sad about having no friends," I say, nudging up closer to her. "You didn't tell anyone what was going on. You pretended everything was okay, but you were having a horrible time at school. I'm sorry. I wasn't a good sister. I didn't see your worry suitcase, because I was so busy worrying about my own."

"It's okay." Topaz blinks and looks down. "Am I a nice person? I mean, those girls said I couldn't be, because Dad wasn't a nice person. They said they wouldn't ever be friends with me and that they didn't like me from the start, and that it proved they were right not to like me now they knew the truth. They said I was boring too."

"Never," I reply. "You're the most interesting person I know. And you're not really terrible."

"What do you mean? Not terrible?"

I'd forgotten I've never actually called Topaz "terrible" to her face. I bluster something about her being amazing and that I meant she's terrific.

"You're the best sister I ever had," says Topaz quietly. When I say I'm the *only* sister she's ever had, she says, "That'll do." Then she says that she's glad we never had to return my telescope. "It's yours and you'll look after it." At that point, I realize Terrible Topaz only got terrible after Dad left. I think it was her way of dealing with it. Like the way I dealt with it by having the worry suitcase. Everybody deals with stuff differently and that's all right. I tell Topaz I love her and she coughs and says, "Same." And I laugh. "I was envious of you, Mabel. Did you know that?" she adds.

I shake my head, confused.

"I didn't like Gavin because I felt left out. I thought you two got on better because you both loved the stars and I didn't fit in. I didn't fit in at home or at school. I felt like an outsider everywhere. It wasn't your fault and it wasn't Gavin's. I took a dislike to him and it was wrong. I didn't look below the surface. I should have listened to you."

I swallow.

"I'm sorry. Gavin helped us when we needed someone," she says. "Gavin was there and I felt happy to have him around then. I really did."

"Me too," I say and I reach for Topaz's arm and squeeze it quickly and she tells me to get off and then we look at each other and burst out laughing. I offer to paint her nails with purple glitter because she still hasn't used that amazing nail polish I got her. Topaz says she's been biting her nails for ages because she was worrying, but she's happy to do anything that makes them look better.

It sounds stupid, but it feels like my suitcase is shrinking. Right now, it's more like a small rucksack.

THE RING

Lots of things have happened in the last few days. The Goblet of Truth is back and has one final crack left. By the way, this was totally confusing to me, because I thought I had thrown the broken pieces of the goblet in the bin. Only, it turned up again under my bed and between Jupiter's claws.

It happened yesterday and it was Mum who found it. She picked it up and looked at it carefully, turning it this way and that. I explained the story behind the goblet and it was magic, and that must be true because it had just escaped from the bin. Next, I told her it was supposed to break when it heard three lies and it was supposed to mend when it heard three truths and when you heard the final truth the cup would mend a broken heart. I told Mum there was one more truth to be delivered.

Mum raised an eyebrow and said she wasn't sure if the goblet was magic at all or could crack when it heard anything, and then she said she thought it looked familiar. Then, without a word, Mum disappeared into the garden shed and a few minutes later she returned with some of Dad's things in a box. It looked like the box my *I Need Space* book had been in. Mum said it was the things that Dad couldn't sell. She'd stored them in the shed. The box still had some books in it and a few bottles of perfume – they smelled horrible, like stinky drains. That's when I noticed a few golden goblets. Some were cracked, some not. Some had two cracks, some had three cracks. They all looked slightly different.

"I think young Jupiter might have dragged a 'gift' into the house, and not just dead ones for once," said Mum. "I think he brought in a goblet or two from our garden shed. That would explain how a new goblet was under your bed after you put the broken one in the bin. And you know what the word Rún means, right?"

"No," I said. "It's just a man's name, isn't it?"

"It might well be. But it also means secret, mystery

or love," replied Mum. She stared at the goblet. "Dad had loads of these ages ago and he was going to sell them, but he didn't because some of them were cracked. We shoved them in the shed."

"And Jupiter brought them in," I said, tapping my finger on my lip.

Mum nodded and said there were plenty more of them lying around. I thought about how the goblet wasn't special and it wasn't magic, because the shed was full of them and they were only ever souvenirs or trinkets you buy at the seafront. I paused for a second. "So Jupiter brought in the first goblet. It was then dropped twice and I think I squeezed it until it broke a third time." My mind whirred like a paper windmill. "Those were the three cracks. It's easy to crack something. After that, I thought I'd left the goblet on the bedroom floor along with my school books but it turned up beneath the bed in Jupiter's claws, so I reckon he brought in another one from the box. I bet, if I look, I'll find the cracked goblet where I left it." Sure enough, there in the corner of my bedroom on the floor, I found the original goblet with all three cracks still in it. "The new one Jupiter brought in only had two cracks. Then I broke that one too when I fell and now he's brought me another new one with only one crack in it."

"Hmm..." Mum looked at me. "I think you're right. You know, there's always a logical explanation if you look hard enough."

I tugged on my earlobe and the words stuttered from my mouth: "I...I...I...don't think it was ever magic. It was never going to mend a broken heart. Maybe I'm silly to believe in stories," I muttered. "You never liked Dad's stories."

Mum looked at me and then said they weren't so bad, when she thinks back. "And it looks like this goblet is the best story of all." She smiled and she didn't look misty-eyed at the mention of Dad and I could've sworn I almost saw her broken heart mending.

Things have been good in our house since Gavin has come back. We've had a lot of fun, taken lots of pictures of us together and laughed a lot. He's here now and we're having a special meal. Gavin wouldn't allow any of us in the kitchen while he was cooking. And now I can see why. When we open the kitchen door, the room is draped with loads of silver stars. They're all different sizes and hanging from the ceiling on threads, all different lengths. The lights are off and the whole kitchen is dotted with tiny tea-light candles which he's placed inside lots of golden goblets from the box. All the candles flicker and throw light on the stars that flutter in the breeze. If ever the goblets were magic, they're magic right now. You can feel it in the air. Something smells lovely and in the background there is soft music playing.

"May I show you to your seat, madam?" Gavin leads Mum to a chair and pulls it out for her and she sits down. He pours her a drink and smiles as Mum says this is amazing. Topaz doesn't look quite so impressed but then she spots a large cake on the side and she looks a lot more interested.

After we've finished eating steaming lasagne that bubbles and squeaks when Gavin sticks in the serving spoon, Gavin brings out a little box and I hear Topaz gasp. Gavin smiles and flips open the lid. Above us a giant silver star rotates and the candlelight catches on a plain metal band inside the box. "It's not an engagement ring," clarifies Gavin. "Your mum and I have discussed that we're not ready for that yet. And there's all the time in the world."

"What are you calling it then?" asks Topaz, leaning over.

"A commitment ring," says Gavin. "My sister told me about them. She said it's a symbol of a relationship that's beginning to develop, maybe into something more serious. Or maybe a promise to love someone." Gavin smiles and adds, "And their family."

I feel my stomach somersault at the word "family" and it feels good.

Mum looks at me and then at Topaz and we both nod. Then she turns to Gavin and grins as he takes the ring from the box and hands it to her. "It's lovely." Mum places it on her middle finger. "It's the most beautiful thing I've ever seen."

"It's a part of the meteorite I found with Mum in 1988," explains Gavin. "I had this piece made into a ring. One piece belonged to Katie, you know, but she wasn't as interested in space as me so she said I could have it. She loved how I had it made into a ring, she thought it made it even more special. She thought *you* must be really special." Gavin gazes at Mum and runs his fingers through his floppy hair.

My eyes grow wide.

"You're one-in-a-billion," whispers Gavin, staring at Mum. Mum smiles and I swear I can almost see the walls around her heart crumble to dust. She tells Gavin she loves it and she loves him. There's a golf ball in my throat as they hug. But at least it's not a worry lump.

"It's hardly a diamond," says Topaz.

"It's a piece of heaven," I reply indignantly. "You can't beat that."

And you can't. Nothing will ever beat the stars.

Later that evening, after we've taken down the silver stars and blown out the candles, we all curl up on the sofa. When I glance up above the fireplace I see that Mum has put a framed photo of us all there, including Gavin. It looks like it's in the right place and we all look happy, even Topaz. As we settle down to choose a movie to watch, Gavin says he'll have to take us to visit his mother, P. C. Wheeler, very soon. He says she might not remember all the stars in the sky these days, but she will always shine like a star to him because we're connected to the stars and nothing will change that. "She'd love to meet you," he says.

"We'd love to meet her too," I answer.

"Sometimes I talk about the world with her, sometimes the stars...sometimes I take her home-made fudge and she smiles. Your mum always has me tasting new varieties and I love to share some of them with Mum." Gavin glances upwards, as if he's remembering something or trying to blink back tears. "Sometimes she asks the same questions over and over and sometimes she gets confused, but I keep talking." His voice cracks. "And there's a lot to juggle and I have to balance Mum's needs with mine, but we still laugh and now we live for the moment."

Mum reaches out and hugs Gavin and then he buries his head on her shoulder and Topaz and me join in and it feels like we hug for ever.

THE BLACK DOG

The day to let our balloons go has arrived. Mr Spooner brought a selection of helium balloons into the classroom this morning and asked us to attach our poems to them with ribbon. We got to choose what balloon we wanted and I picked one that looked like a silver star.

"I know you all put a lot of effort into this project and I'm so happy with the work you've done. That is what makes it special. The real you shouldn't be hidden beneath the surface, the real you is about to fly. And what's more, someone will find your words and they'll touch their lives too. We're all part of a great big family." Mr Spooner is giving us one of his epic speeches and, for once, everyone is listening. He tells us that we're going to the playground and he reminds us that Dolly-Rose won the competition so her balloon should go first. "I hope your teeth survived all the sweets," adds Mr Spooner.

Dolly-Rose reaches into her school bag and brings out a plastic bag and sets it on the table, saying she didn't eat the sweets. "I saved them for everyone," she says. "I thought it was a joint project and winning was good enough. Um...I ate the flying saucers though. I hope that's okay."

Mr Spooner laughs and says kindness costs nothing and it's more than okay and he takes the bag, telling us all to reach inside and take a sweet before we go to the playground, thanks to Dolly-Rose. Then he leads us outside the school and tells us to welcome the parents, who are walking towards us. We're each holding our balloon, coloured ribbons fluttering in the breeze. I smile at Mum, who is standing beside Gavin, who has Nova in his arms. Nova is his new baby niece (named after a star that increases in brightness) and he's looking after her today for Katie (who we're no longer calling Blonde Ponytail Woman because we met her last week and she's definitely lovely and suits the name Katie best of all).

Mr Spooner lets us read our poems one by one and when we're finished he says he was going to do the countdown but he'd originally asked if there was anyone famous or with an important job who could do it, and so is there any parent present who would like to do the honours?

I swallow.

Dolly-Rose's mother steps up and I recognize her immediately. I gasp for a second, thinking that she's not a brain surgeon and this could be awkward, but I needn't have worried. She grins at Mr Spooner and says, "I have the most important job in the world." Mr Spooner waits patiently for the answer. "I am a mum," she says. Everyone claps (except Lee, who is mumbling that Elvis would be better) and Mr Spooner agrees and asks her to do the countdown. When she reaches number one, Dolly-Rose lets her helium balloon go and all the rest follow straight afterwards.

"Poetry in (e)Motion," shouts Mr Spooner as they float upwards and then disappear like tiny coloured boats bobbing over the horizon of a big ocean. Except Lee's – his gets caught on a tree. But he doesn't mind and says it's a fitting end for the bluebottle!

When we're finished and our visitors have gone, we turn to go back to the classroom. Dolly-Rose sidles up beside me and I tell her that I liked her poem about the Black Dog and I loved what her mum said earlier and I was sorry that we weren't the best of friends. I tell her I was wrong to judge her by what I saw on the outside. Dolly-Rose says she's sorry too.

"What for?"

"I stole your cup but I put it back again." Dolly-Rose looks at me and she shakes her head, saying she's sorry over and over again. "I was wrong."

I give Dolly-Rose a little smile. "I don't need the goblet anyway because...um...there are a few others." I think of Dad's box back at home. "If you want, you can have one. I've got plenty."

Dolly-Rose seems startled and doesn't speak for the longest time. "It's okay," she eventually manages. "And I am sorry I took the cup. I only meant to borrow it for a bit. Like I borrowed the book on the goblet too. I only kept the goblet less than twenty-four hours. I put it straight back as soon as I got a chance."

"But why did you want it?" I tuck a stray strand of hair behind my ear.

"Because it had the power to make everyone happy, of course." Dolly-Rose chews on her lip for a second before adding, "I didn't want anyone to be sad ever again."

I stare at Dolly-Rose and my words pour like syrup off a spoon. "When you say you wanted to make everyone happy – do you mean you? Is your heart sad? If you wanted to mend it you should have said. I'd have let you take the goblet right away. I wouldn't have minded."

Dolly-Rose drags her foot along the gravel and makes a tiny hillock of stones. "No, I didn't want to mend *my* heart," she says. "I borrowed it to help my mum."

It feels like I've got a lump of jelly sitting in my throat and no matter how many times I swallow it won't go down.

"I've been lying, you know. We don't live in Buckingham Place. We used to live there, before my dad lost his job. Now we live on the Bluebell Estate, but it's okay there – it's just a smaller house, and Dad says good things come in small packages. I didn't want you or anyone else to know because I thought you'd laugh at me."

I say, "I'd never do that."

"The stories about Mum being a brain surgeon and Dad being a nuclear scientist weren't quite the truth. Mum is a tiler, you're right. And Dad fixes cars now. Anyway, I borrowed all my ideas from that book I was reading, *Daydreaming Daisy*. The girl in the book imagined she had a dad who was a nuclear scientist and a mum who was a brain surgeon..."

I say that a tiler is a cool job. "Your mum is proud of you. You could tell from the way she looked at your balloon floating away," I offer. Tears spring from Dolly-Rose's eyes and she says she's proud of her mum too and she shouldn't tell fibs about her home life.

"That's what I do," mumbles Dolly-Rose. "I like to daydream, like Daisy in the book. You said your dad told stories and that's what I did too. I read lots of books and did lots of daydreaming. And those daydreams helped me escape from the worries I had..." The words trail off and I realize that Dolly-Rose's daydreams were like my worry suitcase – a way for her to deal with her worries. "Only sometimes I'd get carried away and make the daydreams sound real," adds Dolly-Rose. "Just like Daisy did. Then I'd believe them myself and get angry if anyone challenged them. I even thought I'd be a star." Dolly-Rose shrugs and I can see a tiny flicker of pain in her eyes.

"I understand," I murmur and my hand reaches out and touches her arm quickly, before I pull it back again.

"Do you?"

"Kind of." I swallow and add, "And you *are* a star."

Dolly-Rose shrugs. "Yeah, a big mass of gas."

"No," I reply. "That was just a silly joke, really. You *are* a star. We all are. We're all made of stardust, because humans have the same kind of atoms as the rest of the galaxy. So, you are kind of a star already."

Dolly-Rose's eyes widen and she smiles. "And you're not annoying, Mabel Mynt with a 'y'."

I give a tiny smile back before adding, "And I'm sorry for going on about your dog too. It was my way of trying to talk to you. I saw you one morning with a black pug and I couldn't figure out why you didn't like your dog."

Dolly-Rose shakes her head. "I think you might have seen me with Doug the pug, but he doesn't belong to me – he belongs to one of Mum's friends. He wasn't ever my dog – I don't have any pets – but that explains the mistake, so don't be sorry. You didn't know. The black dog I've been talking about isn't really a dog."

I'm confused. Not even a dog? What does she mean?

Dolly-Rose explains that it's a name her mum sometimes uses for depression – she says she's being visited by the black dog. "I overheard her say it on the phone once when I wasn't supposed to be listening. Mum's black dog used to visit us when we lived in Buckingham Place too. He visited us when Dad got made redundant and then he went away but came back when Dad started fixing cars and he even visited when we moved house. He can arrive any time. I don't like him because he makes Mum sad but it's more than feeling unhappy and fed up for a few days, you know. I wanted to help Mum with the magic goblet, but even though I borrowed Mr Spooner's book to read about it and then took the goblet, it didn't work."

I pause. "I don't think this goblet works for anyone. It turned out it's just a cup from our garden shed. My cat brought it in and we have loads of them." I shrug. "I'm sorry, Dolly-Rose. You can still have one though. I promise I'll bring a cup in for you. Then you can keep it."

Dolly-Rose says it's okay, she doesn't want the goblet anyway, because her mum is getting the help she needs now and she's talking about things more. "I'm getting support too. We're all talking about it. Dad said it's important not to keep everything bottled up. The black dog might still come back, no matter where we live or what we do, but Mum says perhaps he'll shrink and then he won't visit as often as before." There's a tiny glimmer of hope in her eyes. "So, you're right, I don't think the cup is for us or was ever for us. But thank you for offering it to me."

"Do you think it would help if you could talk to a

friend sometimes?" I think about how that's helped with my worry suitcase.

Dolly-Rose shrugs. "I don't have any."

I smile. "You've got me."

THE FINAL TRUTH

The latest Goblet of Truth remains on my dressing table beside my piece of the meteorite from Gavin. It still has one crack and Jupiter hasn't brought in any more (although Mum says she found one in her pants drawer). I don't believe in its magic now but even so, a tiny part of me can't help but wonder... So I stare at the single crack in this particular cup, thinking: *What would have been the final truth, if there ever was one?* I swallow. The crack is never going to mend because now I know the cup wasn't anything special in the first place.

I shake my head and pad over to the bookcase,

where I take down my new copy of *I Need Space* by Patricia Carina Wheeler. After Gavin posted it to me I put it straight on my bookcase beside the copy that Dad gave me. Both alongside each other. Both very important to me.

Sitting on my bed now, I'm bathed in a silver wash of moonlight as I turn the first page and let my finger trace the signature at the front: *Patricia Carina Wheeler*. I stare at each page like I'm seeing them for the first time, drinking in Andromeda and Sirius and Cassiopeia and all the other stars and constellations. "One day I'm going to be an astronomer, like you, Patricia Carina Wheeler," I whisper. "One day I'm going to chase my dreams through the galaxy. And no matter what space rocks come hurtling my way, no matter what object tries to stop me, I will *never* give up on my dreams."

I close the book and hug it tight to my chest and that's when I realize now is the time to really move forward. I have two copies of *I Need Space* now and both mean such a lot to me in my life. *Dad* means so much to me and I can't leave him behind. I'm not moving forward without him, so I'm going to write to him. I wasn't ready before but now I am. The time has come. I set the book down and take a sheet of paper and write:

Dear Dad,

For the longest time, I missed you and I worried that we didn't fist-bump at night and we didn't say I love you. I worried that it was my fault. I worried that I had a space in my heart where you used to be. I worried about everything so much it felt like I was carrying around a suitcase. It's a long story, and I'll tell you about it one day, but for now the suitcase is more a small rucksack and if it gets heavy we all talk about our worries so they get a bit lighter. I don't ever want the suitcase to come back.

Over the last few weeks I've wanted to tell you so many things, like how I've grown taller and discovered more about the stars and that one day, when I'm older, I'm going to do work experience in the local observatory. I've been sometimes sad and sometimes happy. Topaz has been sad too, but now she's happy (most days). She used to bite her nails but now they're beautiful. She also used to read romance books. Mum's friend, Gavin, gave her a big box of new books as a gift - there were loads of them which he'd picked himself. But Topaz said she wasn't reading romances any more, because she wanted to concentrate on being a manicurist – that's what she wants to do when she grows up.

I miss you, Dad. I miss talking about the silly things you bought and the fun we had when we went out for picnics. I miss it all.

But I know now that even though you're not within my reach at the moment I haven't lost you for ever and maybe it's okay for me to move forward without worrying. That's what Mum says. I want to move forward and go on a new journey and this time I don't need to take a suitcase with me.

Mabel x

This afternoon there is a letter back from Dad. It is sitting on the hallway table, waiting for me. My hands tremble as I take it to my bedroom. Carefully, I peel it open and inside I can see Dad's writing and all these feelings whoosh inside me as my eyes scan the first sentence.

Dear Mabel...

My heart begins to pitter-patter like the beginnings of an April shower.

I'm sorry I didn't get in touch sooner...

I wanted to, but I felt terrible about what I had done and how I have messed everything up. And I am sorry. Truly sorry. Forgive me. I'm still your dad and always will be. Nothing can change that. I wouldn't let it. I'm still the person who told you bedtime stories and I'm still the same person who carried you on my shoulders. I did something stupid and I'm paying the price. I should pay the price. When you do something wrong, you should hold your hands up and say you're sorry and admit you made a mistake. We all make mistakes – some big ones, some little ones. I made a big one. And it was worse because it took me away from the people I loved and that was my family. In your letter, you said you thought things were your fault. They never were and I'm sorry that you ever believed that. If only we'd told you the truth at the beginning, then perhaps you wouldn't have felt that way.

My heart is beating faster and harder as I read the words.

I didn't face up to it at first, but now I know that keeping you out of my life is a mistake for you and for me, because I miss you and Topaz.

My eyes are raining now.

None of this was ever your fault. Not ever. As a parent I love you, no matter what. There isn't anything you could do to stop me loving you. If you didn't say the words, it doesn't matter. The absolute truth is: even if the words are unspoken, a parent knows how much their child loves them. And that parent loves their child in return. Words unsaid will not break the bond of love. Love is never lost.

One more thing. I hope you always go on a journey, I hope your life is one amazing journey, but travel light, my Mabel. Why carry a suitcase when you've got everything you need in your heart? A heart that might have had a space in it for a while, but I hope you understand that the space can now be filled with love. Keep listening to your heart! I love you!

Dad x

Splashetty-splash-splash-splashetty-splash. The teardrops fall on Dad's letter. I hear a soft buzzing inside my ears and I don't know if it's my heartbeat or the goblet on my dressing table healing.

"The 'absolute truth'. That's the same as the final truth," I whisper, glancing over at the goblet, only I don't get up to look at it. I don't need to. "And I know what that is now. I knew it all along. It's that love is never lost." My heart feels fit to burst and my eyes prickle with more tears. Right now, I feel like the rucksack of worries isn't even a rucksack – it's nothing more than a small purse. "Love is never lost. Not when it's all around us and bigger than the entire universe," I say, wiping away a tear that is dangling from my jaw. The purse is manageable and the worries are manageable and I can go anywhere now without dragging them along with me. Slowly, slowly, I feel the space in my heart begin to fill, like a bath filling with water. I swallow. This is what it feels like to be loved and happy. And I am. One hundred per cent happy.

From now on I'm going to talk through my problems, because I never want a worry suitcase again. I feel okay that the suitcase has turned into a purse and hasn't gone away completely, because I know that's it's only human to have the odd small worry and even then, I can chat about it. Because I'm going to recognize that other people can have worries, just like me. And I'm going to share those worries of mine and I'm going to listen to their worries too.

I still have a list of things inside my head, but this time they are things that I know about my worry purse, and they don't weigh on me nearly so much:

1. It is mine
2. It still might carry the odd worry
3. I can speak to people about the worries
4. No one else can see the purse but it doesn't matter
5. I can't even see the purse but that's okay
6. I am not alone with the purse
7. Other people will listen and understand
8. I can make the purse smaller
9. The purse can get lighter
10. I can carry the purse but if I forget to carry it it's okay.

It's nearly dinner time and I'm in my bedroom, flicking through my notebook. My eyes fall on the page where I've written "The Worry Suitcase". Scanning the poem until I get to the last verse, I touch the paper with my finger and I feel my mouth whisper "No, that's not how this is going to end." I jump up and find a pen and score the poem out before rewriting it:

The suitcase was clever
I thought: It won't go
It's staying for ever
Now I know that's not so
Yes, the suitcase was mine
But now we're apart
The worries have lightened
And love fills my heart

Snapping the book shut, I head over to the window and stare out at the sky. The moon is full and the sky looks like it has been splattered with millions of stars, and the street lamps create halos of light all the way down Bristo Road. I gaze far out across the world and my heart feels full, like the space that was once there doesn't exist at all. And although there are zillions of stars above me, I realize I'm content being here on earth. Right where I'm supposed to be, right here and right now. And not worrying *all* the time.

There's a tiny clink from the gate and I look down, my forehead pressed against the glass. A dark figure shuffles along the path, all muffled up in scarf and hat, and I remember my dream. For a second, I think about the weight of the worry suitcase, but it doesn't land on me. Instead, I inhale and look down and the figure looks up at me and waves and I wave back.

"It's Gavin," I yell.

A couple of minutes later, there's a tap at my door and Topaz comes in and joins me at the window. "Are you coming down? Gavin's just turned up and he's brought fish and chips." I nod as Topaz adds, "He really is one hundred per cent nice. You were right, Mabel."

I laugh. "I asked you this once before and you didn't answer. Do you like cheese strings or strawberry laces?"

Topaz smiles and says we're having fish and chips but if she had to pick... "I like both. I think the world would be boring without either of them."

I nod and gaze up at the pretty sky and Topaz hooks her arm through mine. Together we watch the stars glimmer and shine on their black velvet blanket. Then she unhooks her arm and turns to face me and says I should tell her all about the stars. Her eyes search mine.

"It might take me a long time," I reply, surprised she's asked.

"Well," replies Topaz, holding her fist in mid-air. She waits. Realizing what she's doing, I grin and tighten my fist and we fist-bump. "We've got for ever," she says.

"Yes," I reply. "We really have."